THE CARETAKER

DAHLIA DONOVAN

EDITING: HOT TREE EDITING

COVER DESIGNER: CLAIRE SMITH

FORMATTING: RMGRAPHX

ISBN-10: 1-925448-91-6

ISBN-13: 978-1-925448-91-7

10 9 8 7 6 5 4 3 2 1

To all the caretakers of the world.

PROLOGUE

TAINE
JULY

"You. Can. Do. This."

The continuously repeated murmuring drew Taine's attention to a young man, casually dressed in jeans and a long-sleeved T-shirt, leaning against a wall giving himself a pep talk. Taine recognised the firm whispering readily enough; he'd done the same type of thing before heading out onto the pitch for an important rugby match. What was the teenager facing that forced him to amp up his courage to such an extent?

Is he a teenager? What's he doing in a hospital hallway on his own?

He looked like one—a mousy one at that. Brown, scruffy hair with a matching almost-there beard, brown eyes, and pale skin with a hint of olive undertones. Taine had a feeling, if he stood beside the youngster, it would be like Jack and the Giant. He had to have at least six inches on him, along with a good sixty pounds or more of muscle.

Taine wondered if he should offer a word of encouragement. Anyone who appeared so distraught in the middle of a cancer ward had clearly received some sort of dreadful news. He lamented his own caring nature, inherited, however improbably, from the Scottish priest who had raised him.

"Nurse Whittle?" A mother Taine recognised from a Welsh children's cancer charity he volunteered for poked her head out of one of the rooms to wave at the young man. "We have a few more questions. Could you come back in now?"

So, not a teenager then.

Taine stood silent while the nurse gathered himself. He squared his shoulders, took a deep breath, and exhaled slowly before striding purposefully into the room, shifting from worried young man to confident medical professional in the blink of an eye. If it hadn't seemed beyond weird, Taine might've wished him luck.

"Mr Aphwa?"

Taine grimaced at the mangling of his Maori surname and turned towards the hospital administrator trying to catch his attention. "Call me Tens, if it bothers you."

Taine Andrew Afoa, occasionally known as Tens to anyone who'd watched him on the rugby pitch, had been abandoned on the steps of a Catholic church in Tain in the Scottish Highlands as an infant. The local priest, Dougal Wilson, had not only christened him but raised him in the parish. The closeness of his name to the village's never occurred to Father Wilson.

The village children did pick up on it rather quickly,

teasing him for his name and his mixed heritage. His Maori father, according to the note left with his infant self, had gifted him with darker skin than was usually seen in the village, and a broader frame. Taine had been rather pleased when he developed both height and muscles early in his teen years. Bullies were cowards, after all.

Knobdobbers.

Older now, Taine had grown to respect and appreciate his name, and he didn't mind the nickname so much. At times, it was better than the mangled versions of Taine or Afoa he'd been called.

"Mr Tens?"

Taine barely managed to restrain his desire to bash his forehead against the wall. He tried to smile politely at the hospital administrator. The tightening around her eyes told him it hadn't quite worked. "How can I help?"

"We've gathered the children in one of the day rooms." She nodded down the hall to a set of double doors. "They've been looking forward to your visit all week."

"Good."

Good? Nothing is good about being in this sterile place. Poor sods.

He put ancient history, the young nurse, and everything else out of his mind. His mission here was a simple one— cheer up the sick children. He forced a smile in preparation.

Wonder if Nurse Whittle plays naughty nurse?

Where the hell did that come from? I'm an idiot and a pervert. The nurse has to be at least half my age.

CHAPTER ONE

FREDDIE

"How many cheesecakes do you think it takes to transition me from merely obsessed to utterly pathetic?" Freddie glanced longingly at the box of traditional Welsh treats. His cat, Bitsy, a silver tabby, hopped up on the kitchen counter to sniff at them. He lifted his beloved pet away from the box of baked cheese pastries. "One more couldn't hurt, could it?"

Bouncing around in his kitchen to the music on his radio, Freddie munched on more pastry than was good for him and read through the latest report from one of his clients. His job as clinical nurse specialist who worked specifically with cancer patients kept him busy. He often brought files home to organise.

The box of cheese pies had been a thank you from the mother of one of his younger patients. He closed the lid to attempt some sort of self-control. Reaching into it to grab one last one proved he had none.

"Stop judging me." Freddie glared at Bitsy, who licked a paw and ignored him. "Typical. *Drewgi.*"

Bitsy hissed at him. She always did when he called her a smelly dog in Welsh. He grinned at her before picking the cat up to dance around the kitchen.

He set her down when her paw swatted him in the face. "Fly, my little furry friend. Fly!"

With his cat disappearing under her favourite quilt on his sofa, Freddie shuffled all the papers together to make space to hop up onto the counter. His summer had been a long one without a break, one filled with new patients, new treatments to organise, and a never-ending chain of people to support emotionally through an undeniably trying time.

Between all that and moving into his new apartment, he had never been happier to see the start of September. The weather had begun to cool. Leaves had just started to change colours beautifully. He felt energised by the hint of crisp air and everything else that came with this time of year.

An hour went by, followed by another while he crosschecked dates for surgeries, follow-ups, and therapy. Being diagnosed with cancer was terrifying enough; Freddie tried to make everything else as painless as possible. It was the least he could do.

It had become his mission in life. He had lost both sets of his grandparents, his uncles, all but one of his aunts, and his only cousin to one form of cancer or another, all over the course of six years. The vile illness had stolen so much from their family—how could he not fight to help others who were suffering as they had?

Setting the files aside for the moment, Freddie kicked around the football on the floor. He spun around his kitchen and living room, sending the ball flying. He froze when a banging echoed from underneath his feet. His neighbour probably didn't appreciate his racing around at eleven at night.

He had been on his own for over a year, but it often slipped his mind that he no longer lived on the family farm. He couldn't bang around in his third-floor flat without annoying his neighbour. *Pity.* Sitting still had never come easily to him.

The Star Wars theme sounding from his mobile phone told him his tad had messaged him. His fathers had similar notifications when they text messaged him—Star Wars for one, and Star Trek for the other. He came by his inner geek quite naturally.

Tad: Your dad wants to know if you're coming home for the weekend.

Freddie: I am home.

Tad: We miss you.

Freddie: You need hobbies.

Tad: We miss you.

Freddie: Shouldn't you be happy you have the farm to yourselves after twenty-four years or more?

Tad: We're finishing up a new batch of cheese.

Freddie: Are you bribing me with cheese?

Tad: Yes.

Freddie: Fine.

The downside of being an only child definitely had to be the overprotectiveness of his fathers. They smothered him with their love. It had taken quite a bit of standing his ground to make a move to Cardiff without them trailing along behind him.

Cancer played a part in that as well. Their extended family had slowly dwindled down to his auntie Anna Rees. She also happened to have been his biological mother.

His fathers had always wanted a child together. They hadn't wanted to adopt, so his Auntie Anna had agreed to be their surrogate, after much convincing from her brother Adam. It had allowed them to pass down the genetics from both sides of the family.

He loved all three of them deeply, but going to primary school had been a nightmare for him. Children could often be cruel, and having two fathers made him stand out in a bad way. Acceptance had come slowly to their small village.

They joked about his aunt being his mother. They teased him about being Jewish. They laughed at his love of cheese.

Who doesn't like cheese?

TwmffatsCheese.

His mouth salivated at the mere thought of a slice of fresh Caerphilly. Or even better, maybe his dad would make cheese pudding for him. The trip to Cornwall seemed far more attractive all of a sudden.

The clock chimed midnight as Bitsy prowled by his feet, hunting dust bunnies. He slumped down on the couch, twisting around to stretch his legs out across the cushions. He drifted off to sleep with one important thing on his mind—cheese.

CHAPTER TWO

TAINE

Since retiring from playing rugby internationally, Taine had found two things that made him happy—jazz and his hamster. He had achieved every accolade possible throughout his career in sports. It had been sad to walk away from it.

Sad in some ways. I won't miss the injuries, or the constant travel, or the invasive attention from media and fans. I definitely won't miss being away from Speedy all the time, poor little hamster.

Speedy had his own shire-themed terrarium mansion. It had far more space than an individual hamster needed. Or so his friends liked to tell him whenever they had the chance.

Father Wilson hadn't been overjoyed with his choice of paths for his life. The man had nudged Taine towards the church, but it hadn't been in the cards for him. He didn't think the Catholic faith had much room for gay, sexually active men in the clergy.

In his heart of hearts, Taine had always expected his adoptive dad to abandon him for his lifestyle. The man had prayed for him and continued to love him. "God judges us. No one else has the right."

Now in his sixties, the priest had dedicated forty-one and a half years of prayers to his adopted son. He continued to do so. Taine would never fault the man for his dedication to either him or his faith.

Taine often tried to imagine what had led his mother or father to abandon him on the steps of the church. How desperate must they have been? He had let go of his anger towards them long ago, finding compassion and gratefulness that they had at least attempted to find a safe place for him.

He still had the letter left within the blanket with him. It had been straight to the point with no flowery words or declarations of love. *"Take care of my son. He's part Maori and part Scottish. I can't have him."*

In his youth, Taine had read shame in those words. Now at forty-two, he could instead offer them the benefit of the doubt. Perhaps his mother or father hadn't wanted him to be completely unaware of his heritage; maybe it had been pride in his ancestry and not embarrassment or resentment that led them to put it into the letter.

Father Wilson had gifted him several books over the years on the Maori people. It had been important to the priest that Taine had a firm grasp on both sides of his biological family.

It had provided him with a foundation for his identity many adopted children weren't lucky enough to have; he'd never been forced to struggle with questions of "who am I" and "where did I come from?"

The Land of the Long White Cloud by Kiri Te Kanawa had become a personal favourite. He kept the signed first edition book with him, one of his treasured possessions. It had led him to another obsession—*moko* or body art.

His adoptive dad hadn't been overly thrilled with the development, but to his credit hadn't voiced any harsh criticism. Taine had tattoos on both arms, which covered not only his biceps but parts of his chest and shoulder as well. His left arse cheek and thigh had its own design of swirls and lines, along with a string of tribal turtles all the way up his spine.

All of his tattoos were tribal with a hint of a modern twist and done by a New Zealand artist who had moved to London years ago. Taine had met him through Boyce "BC" Brooks, a fellow rugby player. They'd grown close, as men who fought together often did.

Even if our fighting happened on a pitch with a ball.

Along with BC, Taine had maintained his friendship with several other retired rugby players. Caddock Stanford lived in Looe with his husband, Francis. Remi Chardin, a Frenchman, had married a Cornish woman and moved there after his own retirement from playing for the French national team. And lastly, Scott "Scottie" Monk had shocked all of them by turning into a Zen master surfer on the Cornish coast after their beloved sport had spat him out for being too old.

He'd been closest with BC. The man had returned a few weeks ago from another jaunt across the world with the new love of his life, Graham Hodson. The younger man was a travel journalist who had only recently recovered from a near-fatal fight with stomach cancer.

The two men would be holed up in BC's inn on the Cornish coast. Taine had promised to make the drive out to see them over the weekend. He still couldn't get over the changes in his old friend.

BC had always been up for a laugh but had never enjoyed traveling or expanding his horizons much beyond European borders. BC Brooks flying? Going across the world? Eating exotic foods? Armageddon would clearly be next.

A chirp drew him out of his thoughts to the terrarium that covered a large portion of the far wall of the living room in his flat. Speedy poked his tanned head out of his cave. It had been designed to look almost identical to Bilbo Baggins's home from *The Hobbit*, one of his absolute favourite novels—and movies, for that matter.

He imagined when most people thought of the sort of pet Taine "Tens" Afoa owned, they'd likely picture some massive, terrifying dog. It might fit their image of him with his six-foot-five frame and muscled body, never mind all of his black and grey tattoos, his greying beard and spiked hair.

His wee hamster usually came as a shock. *I don't know why. He's such a loveable little bugger.*

"What do you think, Speedy?" Taine strode over to crouch in front of his furry friend. "Want to take a trip to the seaside? It would be very, *very* British of us."

Speedy squeaked.

I'll take that as a yes. I hope it's a yes.

"No pissing in the Bentley." Taine had made few luxury purchases with the money earned over the course of his career. His silver Bentley Falcon had been his largest splurge. "I could do without having to clean up little pellets from the leather seats."

Speedy squeaked again.

"Hope that's a yes."

Bollocks.

CHAPTER THREE

Saturday morning dawned incredibly brightly and intensely early. Freddie consoled himself in the knowledge that in a few hours he would have cheese. *All the cheese. So much cheese.* He'd also be able to play his bagpipes freely without anyone around to complain. His dads loved him too much to whinge about it.

The weekend in Cornwall would also allow him a chance to catch up with several of his post-surgery patients. He tried to keep tabs on them even after his contract with them had wrapped up. He cared—sometimes too much for his own emotional stability.

After seeing to Bitsy's needs, Freddie grabbed his bag and headed out the door. He'd learned the hard way not to bring his cat to the farm. She tended to chase the animals, leave hairballs in his dads' bed, and make a nuisance of herself.

Stepping out of his flat to find his bright green Mini Cooper vandalised hadn't done much to improve Freddie's already exhausting week. His plan to head out to Cornwall early would have to be momentarily derailed with a call to the authorities to file a complaint; he would never allow anyone to get away with such a visual and criminal demonstration of hatred.

Coc y gath.

His dads would be livid. They'd tried to argue against his moving permanently to Cardiff. He had no doubts they'd add this to their ever-growing list of reasons for him to return to the safety of the farm.

Cardiff in general had been incredibly welcoming and open to him. The only negative standouts were the two twits who shared a flat on the ground floor of his building. They always harassed him—or anyone, really, who didn't fit into their view of the world. It had gotten bad enough the landlord had installed CCTV cameras all over the property.

In some ways, Freddie admired their dedication. They'd managed to carve vitriolic, hateful words all over the doors on both sides of his beautiful little car. *Twmffats.* He couldn't even bring himself to repeat the hurtful language.

It took over an hour to get everything settled with the police and his landlord. Freddie had texted his tad to say he'd be late, leaving out the reason why. It might only be delaying the inevitable, but he could only handle so much at one time.

They'd find out. Freddie couldn't exactly get the damage

buffed away in an instant. To further prolong the pain of their smothering comfort, he decided to drive out to the Fisherman's Refuge on the cliffs along Whitsand Bay to check up on one of his patients.

One of the upsides of his job had to be getting paid to travel around Wales, Devon, and Cornwall. Freddie made frequent trips to visit his clients wherever they lived. He spent more time in his car than he did the hospital, his flat, or anywhere else really.

After a quick stop at BBs for a muffin and an iced coffee to soothe his temper from the early morning adventure, Freddie made his way towards the M4 to start his three-hour drive. Traffic was surprisingly light for a Saturday. He made the journey in record time, pulling up the drive to the inn only to find a massive silver Bentley SUV blocking his path.

Pretentious, rich arse.

He whacked his hand against the horn twice, chuckling at how the jaunty beep didn't match his annoyance. He stuck his head out the window to hurry things along. "Oi! Could you move?"

A wave of a hand through the tinted glass followed the Bentley turning to the right into an actual parking spot and away from the single lane entrance. Freddie pulled up beside it and stepped out of his Mini Cooper. He walked around the vehicle only to find himself face to chest with a Samoan god.

A gravelly chuckle told him that he'd said it out loud.

Cachu hwch.

His embarrassment faded when he spotted a furry creature on the man's impressively broad shoulder. "Is that a hamster?"

"Speedy." Mr God reached up to gently caress the tiny hamster's head.

"He's fast?"

"His name." He smiled, revealing perfect teeth in a crooked grin with his full lips only barely visible through his mostly grey beard. "Speedy the hamster."

Freddie had to laugh at it. "My cat's named Bitsy."

"Is it small?"

"Not anymore." He joined the handsome man in his burst of laughter, waiting until they settled down to offer his hand. "Freddie Whittle."

"Taine Afoa."

Freddie mulled the name over in his mind while trying to remember where he'd heard it and seen the man. He looked so familiar. "So, actually Samoan?"

"Part Maori."

"And apparently part god." BC drew Freddie's attention, sounding far too amused. He'd apparently been standing on the step with his inherited Yorkie, Zeus, at his feet. "I thought you weren't coming until next weekend. Ginger Spice is out on the bluff."

"I'll make my way out to see him." Freddie gave a cheerful wave to Taine when it suddenly dawned on him where he'd seen the man. He'd been one of the sports stars to visit the hospital's children's ward recently. "Have a good day, Speedy—and Speedy's pet."

"Did he just call me a pet?"

Freddie opted to allow BC to answer the likely rhetorical question. He jogged up the hill at the rear of the inn to find

Graham—his patient and friend—on his normal bench. The redheaded journalist shifted over to give him a place to sit. "How've you been?"

Graham slouched down further in his seat. "Hair's almost finished growing back. Thank God. Itched like a bastard, even my bollocks. How come no one ever talks about how you lose all your hair? Not just the stuff on your head."

"*Twmffat.*" Freddie snorted loudly. Those sorts of remarks had been precisely why the man had moved from simply a client to a friend. "Everything else good? Aside from itchy bollocks? I can probably find you a cream for that problem."

"Arse." Graham elbowed him in the side. "I'm doing much better, nothing to worry you or Dr Genevieve. How's she doing with the move to Cardiff?"

"Brilliant. She loves her new office. I'll be turning over some of my Cornwall patients over time, since I'm based out of Cardiff and not Plymouth anymore." Freddie had argued quite adamantly to keep from simply having his patients ripped away from him. He'd slowly transfer them to a new nurse over the course of the next six months. "Any concerns at all?"

"Yes. How about you tell us about the nasty words scratched into the side of your car?" BC had apparently walked up behind them with the bracing wind masking his steps. He loomed like an angry avenger at their backs. "Whose arses are Tens and I kicking? I haven't had a good fight in ages."

"No one's arses are being kicked by anyone. The authorities are handling it fine on their own." Freddie frowned over his shoulder at the retired rugby player. "Tens?"

"It's what we call him. Not sure how he feels about it." BC threw an arm out to whack Taine on the chest. "This numpty made a name for himself by always finishing his runs in practice a good ten seconds faster than everyone else. *Show-off.*"

"Lazy knobdobber." Taine's eyes glittered dangerously in the bright Cornish sun, with almost a golden tint to them. "So, you know who messed up your car?"

"Hamster whisperer," BC shot back at his old friend, disrupting the conversation again.

Freddie couldn't help lifting his eyebrows while staring blankly at the bickering former rugby stars. "Hamster whisperer?"

"Well, look at him." BC nodded towards the small creature huddled against Taine's neck. "Bet he's getting poo pellets all down his shirt."

"*BC.*" Graham choked on a laugh.

Freddie turned towards the redhead. "And you're voluntarily staying with the overgrown child?"

Graham winked at him. "Have you seen the size of his shoes? You know what they say about that?"

"Bet he's got really stinky feet." Freddie glared at BC when he flicked him on the neck. "*Dim gwerth rhech dafad.*"

"Don't go throwing your Welsh insults around." Graham's eyes narrowed on him. "What's this about your car?"

"Just a few local lads who thought they were clever. They weren't."

Taine's strong hand landed on Freddie's shoulder and gave it a squeeze. "Don't allow the bastards to get you down."

"I never do." Freddie blinked back tears at the gentle comfort from the giant of a man. The emotion clogged up his throat, making him strain to get the next words out. "Thank you."

CHAPTER FOUR

TAINE

Speedy did not approve of windy days, yappy dogs, or BC. The hamster had bitten his friend's finger before crawling into Taine's collar and promptly going to sleep. *Typical.* He brought him on an adventure and the creature slept through it.

His little friend had far more in common with Father Wilson than he thought. Taine had once taken the priest on a trip to Rome to see the Vatican. The man had napped through the majority of it.

"Into younger men now?" BC bumped elbows with him before hopping over the bench to sit next to his lover. "I *definitely* approve."

"What're you going on about now?" Taine folded his arms across his chest and glared down at the chuckling idiots.

"Don't start—either of you."

"Saw you watching Freddie's arse when he left." Graham sat cross-legged on the bench with a grin of pure mischief on his face. "He's a nice enough bloke, for a happy bunny."

Taine couldn't quite picture it, having seen the nurse at the hospital with the weight of the world on his shoulders. "A happy bunny?"

"Cheerful. So cheerful it hurts my eyes."

"He's responsible for keeping up the spirits of patients with potentially terminal cancer. I imagine if he came in like a grump, it wouldn't do much to help." Taine had no idea why he suddenly wanted to defend a young man he'd only recently met. He'd never particularly cared for dismissive humour. *Yes, that's it.* Freddie being attractive and having sad puppy-dog eyes had nothing to do with it. "I wasn't watching his arse."

"Right. Go on, pull the other one," BC teased him.

"Why am I subjecting myself to your special brand of absurd shite?" Taine allowed the brisk breeze to wash over him, taking the edge away from his slowly rising temper. The cruel words etched on Freddie's car had angered him, more than he initially thought. They were callously hateful and intentionally hurtful. He breathed in the sea air and let the rage fall away like the waves crashing on the rocks below. "You never said why I had to make the trek out from Cardiff."

"The Sin Bin."

"What?" Taine stepped around the bench, so he didn't feel as if he were frowning over the shoulders of the two men. "What about the sin bin? And why are you saying it so dramatically?"

"His *brilliant* idea." Graham wound up being pushed off the bench by BC. "Plonker."

BC shushed both of them with a sharp clap of his hands. "How many of our friends have either voluntarily or not so voluntarily been forced to retire from their beloved rugby? We get kicked off our teams, and they quickly forget about us, aside from the occasional video clips shown on pundit shows."

"It's a tragedy—getting old and having to stop careening into one another on a rugby pitch." Graham dodged the kick aimed his way and shifted up to reclaim his seat. "Quit it."

"Too many of us have lost our careers. Why?" Taine couldn't quite see where this was going. "What about it?"

"I thought we might all start a workshop together where we teach youngsters the finer points of the game. We can call our company the Sin Bin. Run it from here in Cornwall, or maybe Cardiff since we're all spread out across this part of the country. Might be fun to put all our combined knowledge together." BC had begun to get more animated with each word. He clearly felt incredibly passionate about his brilliant plan. "Remi, Caddock, myself, you, Scottie, and maybe a few others. I've asked everyone to come out to the inn for the weekend. We've enough room to put you all up."

"You're serious?" Taine didn't know if it was genius or idiotic. *Both, definitely a bit of both.* "Not the worst plan you've ever had."

"What is the worst one he's had?" Graham grinned over at the man sitting beside him, who shook his head violently at Taine. "Well? C'mon, spill it."

"Cowpats." He smirked at the scowling BC.

"What?" Graham blinked at him. "Cowpats?"

"Indeed. Your man there decided to cover the manager's office with them." Taine hadn't even needed a second to consider it. "Not sure it helped him get back on the pitch, though, did it?"

Leaving the couple to tease one another, Taine strode up the hill to stand at the edge of the cliff. He tuned out the sounds around him to consider BC's idea. *The Sin Bin.* A fitting name, given the amount of time all of them had spent in the penalty box.

Trouble being, it might not send the right sort of message to those attending. Did they want impressionable youths to think they encouraged bad behaviour on the pitch? Would anyone even want to attend with that sort of name?

"Attend our rugby workshops on how to get your arse thrown off the pitch in record time."

Maybe the concept could use a little work—or a lot.

He supposed some of their behaviour likely spoke for itself. *Not mine, of course.* Aside from one infamous incident early in his career, his reputation had always been impeccable. He'd been the standout, along with Remi, while the rest of the group of friends tended to get themselves into trouble far too frequently.

"He's thinking—careful not to disturb the frowning beast." BC's loud whisper carried over on the wind. He threw an arm over Taine's shoulder when he reached him. "Well?"

"Idea needs work, maybe the name as well." He shoved the grinning idiot away from him. "Not convinced we can all work together without a few bashed skulls."

"Wouldn't be the first time."

"True." Taine couldn't disagree with him. They'd been kicked out of enough pubs in their younger days. "Definitely not convinced about the name."

"What's wrong with the Sin Bin?" BC asked stubbornly.

"Sounds like a brothel." Taine shifted Speedy slightly. He'd have to put the hamster back in his travel terrarium at some point. "Or a grungy pub in a back alley in the worst part of town."

"Told you," Graham crowed cheerfully from the bench.

"I'm ignoring you both." BC gave them both a one-fingered salute. "Would it kill you both to be a bit more sodding supportive?"

"Yes."

Taine couldn't help sharing Graham's grin. "Probably."

"Fuckwits." BC glared before breaking into a chuckle. "Caddock will agree with me."

"You really want to call it the Sin Bin?" Taine didn't think it sounded much like the name of a training course. "What if we started our own pundit podcast? It would fit the title you're so insistent on."

BC turned serious, an unusual look for the usually jovial man. "Not a bad idea. Didn't you go on a podcast with those two blokes from Liverpool? Or was it London?"

Taine had been introduced by Remi to two rugby fans that ran a successful weekly podcast. He'd been interviewed by them twice. "London."

"We'll talk about it with the others." BC turned to lead him down the hill towards the inn. "I still like the Sin Bin."

"You would."

CHAPTER FIVE

FREDDIE

In the short drive from the Fisherman's Refuge to his family farm outside of Launceston, Freddie had plenty of time to consider the Maori god with the hamster, tattoos, and deep voice. The man's strong hand on his shoulder had left an impression, though not necessarily a visible one.

Dating had been practically impossible as a teenager. Not many had wanted to brave the disapproval of Mr Whittle and Mr Rees—now Mr Whittle and Mr Whittle, since they'd finally been able to marry when the law had changed. They'd been intimidating, to say the least.

He hadn't had much luck since leaving home either, so maybe his parents hadn't been the issue. With his constant driving to see patients, finding a man to go out with hadn't exactly been a high priority on his list of things to do. He barely managed to make it beyond a second or third date.

And sex.

Sex.

Freddie hadn't quite managed to do more beyond orally pleasuring a few of those dates. *I'm a virgin. I'm twenty-six and a virgin. I am pathetic.* It would've only been worse had he still been living in his childhood bedroom.

Is it wrong to pray for the right first partner?

He didn't necessarily feel his first time should be something monumentally special. His virginity wasn't exactly some mystical treasure to be gifted to his one and only love. *Right, no more reading Auntie Annie's romances.* He simply didn't want to rush into something only to regret it later.

The closest thing Freddie had to a relationship had been with Tristan, who he had been with for almost eight months. He'd experienced his first brush with something akin to love. Stars had definitely filled his eyes whenever they went out together.

When Freddie refused to immediately fall into bed with Tristan, the bastard decided to find someone who would. He'd found him screwing around with one of the part-time workers at the farm. They'd been visiting for a three-day weekend.

His fathers quickly kicked both the worker and Tristan out of the farm on their arses. Freddie refused any calls from the man after. It only served to cement his belief in not rushing into a sexual relationship.

The image of Fred and Adam Whittle chasing two young

men off their property would stick with Freddie for a long while. It almost made up for his slightly bruised heart. His fathers really could be intimidating when they wanted to be.

None of their family were particularly tall or broad. Freddie had inherited his lithe muscles and lanky body from both sides. His thick brown hair had come from the Whittles. The slight tint of colour to his skin came from his Jewish heritage.

The Rees family had come over to Wales in the early 1900s after facing the destruction of their previous lives, changing their last name from Reizen to blend into their new home. Freddie remembered his grandparents telling stories about their emigration from Russia. It had always made him appreciate his own life more.

Perspective.

Always important to have.

The Whittles had deeper roots in Cornwall. They were farmers who had made and sold cheese for close to two hundred years, a long history Freddie had always felt proud to be a part of. Being able to eat a mountain of free cheese had only been an added bonus.

I do love my cheese.

A honking horn drew his attention from delicious treats to the fact that he'd almost missed the turn into the farm. Freddie waved at Uncle Graeme when he drove by him. The man worked on the Whittle farm during the busy months of the year. He'd have taken the mickey for weeks if Freddie had actually missed the turn.

Bastard.

"Adam. Adam. He's here. Our Freddie's home."

Freddie could hear his dad yelling for his tad before he'd even stopped the car or shut the engine off. He smiled brightly at the two men in their fifties who stood with an arm around each other by the front door of the farmhouse. *How can I be annoyed, even if they're acting like they haven't seen me in years instead of weeks at most?* He offered them a cheerful hello in his tad's native tongue. *"S'mae."*

"Frederick, the junior." His dad and namesake stormed across the gravel path to stop by the racing green Mini Cooper. He didn't even turn to offer Freddie a hug when he stepped out. His finger shook as it reached out to point towards the damage on the door. The afternoon sun highlighted the edges with annoying clarity. "Who. Did. This?"

His tad moved over to crouch down to get a better view of the hatred carved into their son's car. "Oh, Freddie."

"I'm fine. It's fine. I'll get it buffed out on Monday." His protests didn't make an impact on his fathers, who crushed him between them in a smothering hug. "Breathing is becoming an issue. I'm serious. Dad? Tad? Anyone? You'll feel awful if I suffocate from a *cwtch*."

"And yet, you're still managing to ramble incessantly while not breathing? Impressive skills. You should put it on your CV." Adam Whittle, his tad, had always had a dryer sense of humour than either Freddie or his dad, Fred. "Did you at least contact the police?"

"Of course he did. Our Freddie's a smart boy."

Freddie wiggled out from between them and tried not to glare at his fathers. "I'm not five years old. I'm quite capable of handling two twmffats who don't have a brain in their heads."

"You were such a darling at that age. You watch your language." His dad went all nostalgic, apparently losing himself in his memories. "I wonder where the family photo albums are. Where did we store them?"

Freddie covered his face with his hands and counted backwards in his head in English, Welsh, and French for good measure. "Not enough cheese in the world to save me from this shit."

"Watch your language."

"Yes, Tad." Freddie wondered if they'd notice if he pulled his hair out. *Shit.*

"Watch your language." Tad sent his son a knowing look.

Nothing could humble a man like having his parents treat him like a toddler. His dads always managed to make him regress to his brief rebellious stage. He'd left home to avoid it.

Rebellious might actually be a bit strong of a word for it. Freddie had simply balked at all the constant coddling. They loved him. He knew it, but wished they'd occasionally not try to drown him in it.

His auntie Anna always told him to be kind to his fathers. She often reminded him of the struggles they had gone through as a gay couple during a time when the world was even less accepting. Their deciding to have a son hadn't made things better.

Not that they would've ever complained. Freddie knew his fathers considered him to be their miracle. He only wished they'd at least acknowledge he had not only grown up, but become a working adult who lived on his own.

"So, cheese?" Freddie wanted to move the conversation

away from his car. Nothing would be solved by harping on it. The world might've improved, but it hadn't magically become completely free of intolerance. His dads, however, remained staring at the vile words. "I'll be inside eating all your cheese."

"Freddie, *love*." His dad's expressive blue eyes pierced his own brown ones. "I hoped you would outgrow your need to hide your hurts from us. We're family, son. We share—the good and the bad. One day you'll learn you don't have to smile for us."

Additional hugs followed, as always, before his dad wandered off with his phone glued to his ear. He appeared to be calling around to see about getting the paint redone. *Typical.* They always—his dad in particular—took over getting things done for him.

When Freddie had moved to Cardiff, he'd fought tooth and nail to manage it on his own. It had been akin to treason when he ignored the apartment listings they sent him. His refusing to use the movers they hired had caused a bit of a family incident; his aunt had intervened to calm the situation down.

She was always brilliant at handling them.

His friends always exclaimed endlessly about how sweet his parents were. *Sweet?* They'd drive him to violence if they didn't stop suffocating him. Was it wrong to want to be treated as a twenty-six-year-old and not a toddler?

"You're in time for tea, *cariad*." His tad threw an arm around his shoulder and guided him towards the farmhouse. "Cheese toast? You can tell me all about your romance troubles."

Coc y gath.

CHAPTER SIX

TAINE

Halfway through the weekend, Taine began to long for the quiet of his own space. Individually speaking, his friends usually managed to behave like relatively intelligent adults, who had some semblance of maturity. Unfortunately for him, when they all came together, it had a tendency to devolve into them behaving like lads in their teens out at a pub for the first time.

With the others playing a rowdy version of charades complete with shots of liquor for anyone who failed to guess correctly, Taine stepped outside to watch the clouds drifting across the moonlit sky. The nights had started to have a distinct chill to them. He almost regretted not having his leather jacket with him—a remnant from the days when he preferred riding around on a Valkyrie to the comfort of his Bentley.

"Beautiful night." Remi joined him outside, though the Frenchie had been wise enough to throw on a coat. He held out a tumbler of what smelled like a smoky whisky. "How's Claire? Are you still seeing her?"

"No." Taine shook his head emphatically. "Not for months."

Remi chuckled darkly after a sip of whisky. "It ended as well as we thought it would. *Merde.* I'm going to owe Caddock. I knew I shouldn't have taken him up on the bet."

"Great friends you are." Taine decided to drown his annoyance with another drink. He hadn't seen Claire in over a year and hoped she'd moved on to someone else. "It ended *brilliantly.* She tried to hamster-nap Speedy. She didn't quite understand why I wouldn't propose after being together for two years."

"Are you not ready for commitment? You've never seemed as terrified of it as BC or Scottie." Remi leaned against the railing, watching the others through the large windows. "Or would you prefer to settle down with a man? I know you've enjoyed both in the past."

"I've loved both men and women." Taine had always found himself equally attracted to both genders with no preference for one over the other. "It's not a case of preferring one. The person matters more to me than what I find under their clothing. Claire was lovely."

"But not the one you wish to spend the rest of your life with?" Remi sounded confident that he understood without needing further explanation. "She wasn't your perfect match."

"My perfect match?" Taine tapped a finger against the rim of his glass before having another sip. He shook his head at the ridiculous nonsense being thrown his direction. "Is there actually such a thing? You're still in the first blushes of marriage. You should talk to me about it in five or ten years."

Remi gave him a mild glare, his Gallic version of disapproval. "How many women have I left broken-hearted before Sarah? I've been more cynical about emotions than all of you combined. My wife? She couldn't be more perfect for me, *because* of all the imperfections in our relationship. Don't mock me until you've felt the raw fear of loving another person more than yourself."

"She's making you soft and swoony." Taine borrowed a word from Caddock's husband, Francis. "Do you miss the chaos of rugby season?"

"Have you met my wife's family?" Remi didn't even blink at the sudden shift of conversation while gulping down his drink. "The Blacks of Boscastle provide enough chaos for me. I do miss the camaraderie off the pitch. I never imagined we would drift so far apart."

"Memories."

"What about them?" He frowned in clear confusion.

"We remind each other of the glory days when our achievements were celebrated by tens of thousands of people screaming our names." Taine often found himself missing the rush of adrenaline that hit right before a match. They'd wait to be called out on the pitch—ready to battle for a win. "No one cares about heroes who've been unmasked and grown too old to rush into burning buildings."

"We played a sport, Tens." Remi grasped him by the shoulder and shook him lightly. "Don't confuse feats of skill on a pitch with actual acts of heroism."

"Perspective?"

"Oi. Get your arses in here." Caddock banged on the window, causing both men to startle in surprise. "It's your turn to humiliate yourself, Tens."

Taine knew it wouldn't be the first or last time he embarrassed himself with them—or in front of them. Their antics had been the stuff of legends. The stewards still hadn't managed to figure out how they'd changed the banners in the stadium to Jolly Roger flags.

Legends.

In our own minds, at the very least.

Two hours later, the group of drunk men stumbled mostly naked down the rocky beach into the below-freezing water. Taine tackled a reluctant Remi, who had refused to remove his boxers, into the ocean. If he was going to die of cold, they'd all die together.

Shite.

It's freezing.

They should've all known better. In his late thirties, Caddock had the dubious claim at being one of the youngest of the group. None of them had an excuse for behaving stupidly or recklessly.

When have we ever had an excuse for it?

Never stopped us before now.

Alcohol had only encouraged them to throw caution to the wind. Or maybe it had been nostalgia for the days before injuries and retirement. Whatever the cause, only a miracle would keep them from having colds by morning. Taine found it hard to regret, even as he huddled under a blanket to get warm.

They shivered together in the den around a roaring fire. Conversation slowly drifted off, age and booze making them drowsy. Taine hoped, with his last thought before drifting off to sleep, that this would prove the impetus for them getting together more frequently.

The following morning the shrill sound of multiple mobile phones ringing brought all of them to the rough realisation that they were too old for hangovers. A blurry, dark image on the cover of a tabloid paper of five retired national rugby team stars bare-arsed and fancy-free on a beach in Cornwall didn't do much to improve their moods. *Shite.* Father Wilson would definitely see it.

Shite.

They all had a giggle—a manly one—more of a chuckle really, over the article and photos. None of their reputations would be damaged by this. *Who cares?* He had a feeling their mutual friends would be teasing them for months and months over it.

"Sarah's going to laugh herself to death when she sees this." Remi sat with his head in one hand while his other clutched at a mug of tea. "Whose bright idea was this?"

Taine nodded his aching head slowly towards BC. "His inn, his whisky, his beach—I blame him."

"Oi! It was Ginger Spice's idea, not mine." The man in question lifted his head from the tabletop long enough to answer before gingerly resting it back down again. "Have mercy. We're too old to get so pissed."

He had a point.

CHAPTER SEVEN

FREDDIE

Since becoming a registered nurse, Freddie had received many strange requests. During his internship working at an A & E, he'd seen everything from the bizarre to the hilarious to the horrifying. Nothing shocked him, not anymore, or so he thought.

Sunday had come rather early for him. Mornings always did on a farm. His grandfather had always loved to say, "There's no rest for the wicked, or for farmers either."

He hadn't been awoken by his fathers, or cows, or anything related to the farm. His mobile had rung with a plea from Graham to return to the inn with anything to help with headaches, vomiting, and potential colds. He'd reminded the man that he wasn't a doctor. It didn't matter.

What on earth have they been doing?

As his curiosity got the better of him, Freddie left a note for his fathers, who were having a rare sleep-in. He snagged a scone and made a rushed cup of tea. He hoped to find a Tesco on the way over to grab a few supplies for the suffering men.

A sorry bunch of adults sat around the table in the kitchen at the inn waiting for him. BC managed a brief introduction of sorts. "Scottie, BC—wait that's me—I mean, Caddock, you know Tens, and Remi—the Frenchie." *Well, they're definitely hung-over.* Freddie managed, only barely, to not bang around. It would've been cruel to add to their self-inflicted pain.

He thought about it, though.

He did.

"You are a god—a happy bunny sort of one." Graham grabbed at the paracetamol, taking it before any of the other men could grab it. "I love you."

"Plonker." BC glared at the redhead before holding his hand out for medicine. "Please, sir, can I have some more?"

"*Twmffats.*" Freddie shook his head and started to dole out medicine where required. He checked temperatures as well as made sure they all hydrated sufficiently. "Aren't you all old enough to know better?"

"Yes."

"No."

A chorus of groaned answers came from all over the kitchen. Freddie had to laugh at them. He glanced over the shoulder of one of them to find him perusing a tabloid article.

"Is that—" Freddie leaned forward to get a closer look. "Oh. My. God."

"Shh." Caddock held a finger to his lips. "Less with the loud, more with the relieving of pain."

"As a member of the medical community, I feel it is my duty to warn you of the dangers of drinking to excess." Freddie raised his voice slightly, hiding his smile at the winces and betrayed glances sent his way. "Also, do you know what hypothermia can do to your private parts? It's not pretty."

"Private parts? Who calls their cock a private part?" Scottie spoke up for the first time, his head still face down on the table, cushioned by his arms. "Are you twelve?"

"Says the grown adult who got himself in a newspaper with his arse hanging out for all to see?" Freddie whacked his hand on the table, sending all the men moaning and clutching their heads. "Oh, I'm so sorry. Are your heads still sensitive to sound?"

"Say you're sorry for being an ungrateful arse." Taine kicked Scottie's chair. "He didn't have to spend his Sunday helping us out. He could've left us to suffer."

"Sorry." Scottie sounded more pained than actually apologetic. "Can I have the fucking pain medication now?"

Freddie set the last of the paracetamol next to him. "*Diawl bach.*"

"I'm hazarding a guess that wasn't a compliment." Graham seemed to be peering at Freddie in a new light. "Any Halls in that bag? My throat's gone all sore."

Freddie plucked out several packs of Fisherman's Friend from the Tesco bag. "Here. These always work better."

"Don't taste better." Graham grimaced.

"And?" Freddie didn't have much sympathy for any of them. He certainly wouldn't put up with bad moods sent his direction.

"It'll help. Trust me."

It took much grumbling, but all the men had finally medicated and hydrated themselves to improved moods. Freddie waved off their invitation to breakfast. He headed towards the door, intent to get back to Launceston before his dads had time to miss him.

They'd ask too many questions, assume too many things about him dashing out in the early hours to help a group of former rugby players. He could lie. They'd see through it, though; they always did.

"Frederick?"

Freddie paused at his full name—no one other than his angry dads called him anything other than Freddie. He paused by the front door to see Taine had caught up to him. "Yes?"

"Thank you, Frederick, for coming out to help us poor sods out."

He had to clear his throat to respond. The man's deep voice saying his name caused his stomach to flip and his lower region to rise in interest. He smiled through it. "I'm always happy to help."

They stood awkwardly. Neither knew what to say. A loud thud was their only warning before a stumbling Scottie slammed into the back of Taine, which sent him into Freddie like a row of dominos tumbling to the floor.

Freddie groaned under the mass of muscle. He cringed inwardly when it dawned on him that Taine would now be able to feel his earlier piqued interest. "Could you get off me?"

"Want me to help you get off?" Taine's murmured comment sent a shiver down his spine. "I wouldn't mind."

"No, I want you to help me get *up* before my ribs decide to cave in completely," Freddie replied tartly, if a bit unsteadily. "What do they feed you rugby types?"

"He's calling you fat, Tens," Scottie teased from somewhere above them. Freddie couldn't see him through the bulk of the man crushing him to the floor. "Up you two get, or I'll start making assumptions that'll have me blushing."

The weight of Taine lifted off him, and a hand reached down to yank him up to his feet. Freddie frowned at Scottie, who hadn't quite removed his fingers yet. The tall, muscled, blond man had an edge to him that was worrying.

"*Scottie.*" Taine shoved his friend down the hall away from them. "Go see Caddock."

"Aye aye, Tens."

"He's—something." Freddie chose to stick with his fathers' advice to not be rude when it wasn't necessary. He glanced up to find Taine's intense gaze focused on him. "I should get going. My dads will wonder what happened."

"Your dads?"

"My family is a modern one." Freddie had no intention of explaining his family to a man he'd only recently gotten to know. "Was there anything else?"

Taine cocked his head to the side as if assessing Freddie. He slowly smiled—a wide, dangerous sort of grin, rather akin to a predator who had just caught his prey. "Can I have your number?"

Pardon?

Not the question I thought was coming.

"Why?" Freddie shook his head at himself. *Do I care why*

an incredibly attractive man wants my number? He internally shrugged before holding his hand out. *No, no I don't care why.* "Give your phone over—I'll add it for you."

The bemused expression on Taine's face made the tingling in his spine at the brush of their fingers worth it. Freddie quickly entered his mobile number under the name Nurse Bunny. He imagined the man would have to go to great lengths to explain it to anyone who saw it.

"Enjoy your weekend with the lads." Freddie started towards the door, tossing the phone over his shoulder. "Don't get too drunk. I'm not making another emergency visit to cure hangovers."

CHAPTER EIGHT

TAINE

Taine could only stare in bewildered amusement from his mobile to the shut front door. "What the shite?"

"Having trouble, Tens?" Scottie joined him in the foyer once again, a smug smile on his handsome face. On the rugby pitch, it had bothered Taine far more than it did now. "Did the baby doctor run off? Time to change his nappies?"

He scratched the underside of his neck where stubble had started to make itself known. *Time to shave.* "Don't be more of an arse than you already are, Scottie. What's your issue with him? He brought something to ease your pain. You should've offered your thanks—not the piss-poor attitude you treated all of us to on and off the pitch every day. You're getting more bitter with every year that goes by. Suck on any lemons recently?"

"Oh, fuck off, Tens." Scottie punched him in the arm, light enough not to take seriously but harder than a joke would've been. "He's a bit young for you to want to bugger him silly."

"Pardon?" Taine found himself stepping forward into Scottie's personal space. He brought a powerful hand up to drop it heavily on his friend's wide shoulder, gripping more tightly than required. "One of these days, you're going to have to get over the fact that you're attracted to other men—we all have. Until you manage to get your head out of your arse, though, stop taking your issues out on everyone else. *Got it?*"

Scottie stepped up to him, shifting forward with his lips twisting from a smile into something darker. "Or what? Aren't you island boys too mild-mannered for anything more than a lecture?"

"Island boys? I'm half Scottish, you knobdobbing shite." Taine might not have the height advantage on Scottie, by an inch or two, but he'd stayed in better shape since leaving the game. His voice deepened and the brogue from his hometown thickened. He pressed Scottie back against the wall, shoving him twice to get his attention. "What's all this going to prove? You should have some tea and calm down before you ruin the only friendships you have left."

"Friendships? Is that what we're calling this?" Scottie's breath held the slightest hint of liquor still. Taine wondered if maybe he'd been drinking long after they'd all gone to sleep at two in the morning. "Right. *Friendship.*"

"Break it up, lads." Caddock made an imposing figure in the shadowy hallway. He ruined the image by flipping on the lights and grinning at them. "Tens is too old for this shit, and honestly, Scottie, you've stared at all of our arses frequently enough—we don't care. Why should you? Though, Francis might send Sherlock after you if you don't quit staring at mine."

Deciding the best course of action would be to leave Scottie's existential crisis to Caddock, Taine ducked around both of them to return to the kitchen. He readily accepted a mug of tea from BC before sinking into one of the uncomfortable wooden chairs with a groan. *Maybe the Sin Bin is more appropriate than I thought.* They'd all matured a little less than he'd initially assumed.

"He means well." BC stood by the large windows covering one wall of the kitchen and nodded towards where they could see Caddock and Scottie walking—and arguing—outside. "I hope."

"He doesn't. He's a right miserable twat." Graham lifted his head up from where he'd been dozing on his folded arms, which rested on the table. "I don't think getting shitfaced was on the list of doctor-approved activities."

BC twisted around to crouch in front of him. "You all right?"

With his tea in hand, Taine made his way through the inn down to the library. He didn't want to intrude on a quiet moment between the couple. Graham had brought out a caring and mature side to BC that none of them had known existed.

It made him miss being in a relationship.

Almost.

None of the books drew his attention; he'd never been

much of a reader. Father Wilson had given up after all of his gifts of books ended up unread in stacks on a shelf. He sat by the fireplace and contemplated the future instead.

Or, he intended to until a beep on his phone signalled a new text message. Remi wanted him to go for a ride into a nearby town to find a decent cup of coffee. *A suspiciously familiar-sounding village.* The Frenchie tended to sneer at anything tea related.

"You couldn't have walked down the hall?" Taine kicked his friend's shoe lightly. "You had to text? Lazy bastard."

"Want to get away from the madness for a few hours? Sarah's off to visit her brother in Boscastle. It's not too far from here—bit more than half an hour at most." Remi sounded anxious to be off. His wife had just entered her second trimester, so Taine couldn't blame the man. "Well?"

Taine had only met Ivan Black once, at the wedding. The Blacks of Boscastle, Sarah's family, had quite the reputation. "You're buying coffee."

"*Merde.*"

The Blacks of Boscastle had been blacksmiths in Cornwall for hundreds of years, Ivan being the latest member of the family to follow the tradition. They had deep roots in the Cornish hills, long memories, and short tempers—if Sarah were anything to go by. She might be short, but her hair, like her anger, ran red and vibrant.

They stopped for coffee once they arrived in Boscastle. Taine wasn't surprised when Remi picked up an extra cup and a treat for his wife. The man doted on her.

"You be nice to my Sarah."

Taine blinked at the mild warning thrown his way when they pulled up in front of the Boscastle forge. "Me? I'm sure you've confused me with Scottie."

Remi narrowed his eyes but finally nodded his agreement. "We're going to have to sit him down to have a chat at some point."

"That sort of chat usually ends with fists and broken jaws." Taine remembered the last chat they'd tried to have with a friend. Caddock had been lost in grief after his brother died and he lost his career to an injury. He'd almost lost himself as well. Taine's jaw still ached from the punch swung his way. "You're in charge this time."

"*Merde.*" Remi reached up to rub his jaw. "Maybe we should let Caddock and BC deal with it."

"Agreed." Remi blew on his coffee before taking a sip. "Someone has to talk to him. He's falling apart at the seams. We're going to see him on the news if we're not careful—beating some poor bugger for looking at him funny."

"Caddock would know all about falling apart." Taine glanced out the window at what looked like a smithy from a century long gone. "This it? Did we step back in time?"

Remi hesitated with obvious unease. "Ivan's not been doing so well. I told you about the accident, right?"

Over drinks before the wedding, Remi had told Taine all about his soon-to-be younger brother-in-law who had, as a young man, been involved in a drink-driving accident. It had caused serious injuries to all three of the lads in the vehicle, Ivan included. The young Black had suffered permanent damage to his short-term memory, amongst other issues.

"I remember."

"He's getting worse." Remi shut the vehicle off and frowned at the man standing outside the forge. Ivan looked like a warrior from the highlands with a permanent storm cloud over his head. "His temper isn't exactly a walk amongst the tulips either."

"*Wonderful.*"

CHAPTER NINE

FREDDIE

If life were at all fair, after the dreadful start to his weekend, Freddie imagined Taine would've reached out to him—at least once. A series of charming texts would've followed throughout the day, all culminating in an invitation to dinner. He hadn't even gotten a brief "here's my number, so you have it" text.

His phone didn't beep once. Freddie wasn't disappointed. He wasn't.

Maybe a bit.

He'd only met the man a few times. There was no reason to be even mildly put out over the silence. His mood, however, remained slightly dented throughout the rest of the morning and into the afternoon.

It plummeted further when Genevieve—Dr Genevieve Williams—sent him an emergency text. The kind that meant a patient had taken a turn for the worse. *Time for Nurse Bunny to hop to it.* He dredged up a smile from somewhere deep inside and went to inform the elder Whittles about his trip ending earlier than anticipated.

His tad followed him out to the Mini Cooper, still scratched up with hateful words. Comforting arms wound around him. "You seem down, *cariad*. Is it more than the vandalism?"

"I'm fine." Freddie turned up the brightness on his smile.

"You usually are."

The arms around him tightened briefly. They stepped back from each other after a moment. Freddie couldn't help a wince at the knowing sympathy in his father's eyes, a gaze that meant to offer comfort.

It served to make Freddie even more tired than he'd been, weary over the fact that his smile hadn't been enough. The drive to the hospital outside of Cardiff seemed to drag for hours and hours.

It might not be Monday yet, but in his soul, Freddie knew the draining workweek had started early for them. One of the nurses on duty handed him a file when he walked down the hall. He already knew exactly where to go.

Little Katie Brown was a bright three-year-old girl who before her chemo had had curly red hair that made her blue eyes stand out even more. Cancer in the young always seemed extraordinarily unfair; his heart had hurt just looking at her medical file, never mind having to work to keep her spirits up—and her parents'.

The parents.

Angry, helpless, impotent in the face of their worst nightmare.

Freddie had seen many of his colleagues burn out in their careers simply from dealing with the families of their patients. He held on by the skin of his teeth, hoping to make at least one person's path easier. His job might not be what cured cancer, but he could work to smooth their journey.

"Fweddie." Katie waved at him from the hospital bed, which always seemed so large it swallowed her up in the crisp white sheets. Her parents had brought in her favourite unicorn quilt to cheer up the room. "Hello, Fweddie, I got pudding."

"Delicious. What flavour, love?" Freddie turned up his smile and bounded over to the bed to sit gently beside her. He took her tiny, frail hand in his. "Can I have some?"

"No, silly. I eated it all up." She sounded inordinately proud of this fact. Given how much chemo affected her ability to eat, it wasn't overly surprising. "Got a new hat. It's got kitty ears."

"So I see." Freddie leaned up to kiss her pink knit hat covered head. "You get some rest, Katie-cat. I'm going to have a chat with your mum and da outside."

Leaving Katie with her brothers and grandparents, Freddie stepped into the hall to speak with the Browns and Genevieve. The latter had made it to the hospital a few minutes before him. They both tended to get called in on the harder cases— the lost causes. They were both too stubborn to give up.

Many long hours followed their initial consultation with the Browns. Genevieve had him searching for specialists who would be open to trying newer treatment methods. Little Katie's cancer had come back with a vengeance, and surgery or a dose of chemo wouldn't do anything to put a dent in it.

Freddie found a moment at four in the morning to grab a cup of tea and a stale scone from the nurses' station. He barely managed to choke down half of it. The lump in his throat made swallowing difficult.

He dumped more sugar into his cup, stirring it woodenly. Something had to keep him going. It wouldn't do to disappoint Katie.

He would end up letting her down. She'd never know it. No one would see fit to blame him.

I will.

I do.

I always do.

Though relatively young in his field, Freddie had always been almost mystically astute at reading a patient's odds of survival. *A sixth sense? Maybe?* Nothing they did would help Katie. He doubted she had more than a few weeks to go.

I'll still fight to give her every moment I can.

"Go home, Freddie." Genevieve took one assessing look at him and snapped the order out without hesitation. "Rest. See Bitsy. And for the sake of my blood pressure, get your car taken care of. If I have to look at those words again, I might go into such a rage that I give myself a heart attack."

"Will do, Gen," he answered on autopilot. He tried to smile; his mouth refused to obey. "Let me know if anything changes."

The drive across Cardiff from the hospital to his flat went

by in a blur. Freddie realised he might be more exhausted than he'd initially thought. He repeatedly yawned on the way up to his flat.

He stopped.

And he stared.

In neon pink, the words on his car had been painted on his front door in terrible penmanship. A note shoved partially under the welcome mat from his landlord indicated the damage would be fixed in the morning. The vandals had been apprehended, for all the good it would do.

I need a new place to live—preferably without the gay-bashing wankers, to quote Graham.

Bitsy met him at the door, rubbing against his leg and meowing for her treat. He lifted her up into his arms and carried her into the kitchen to put out her favourite snack—tuna. She happily hopped onto the counter to indulge.

After forcing himself to eat something more substantial than a scone, Freddie collapsed on his couch with a groan. He turned on his telly to watch *Doctor Who,* since the DVD set was still in his PlayStation. Bitsy climbed up on his chest to doze with him. He started to drift off while the doctor ran through time with his companions.

He glanced down at his right wrist to read the quote tattooed there. "Courage, dear heart."

I'm going to need all the courage I can muster.

CHAPTER TEN

TAINE

"On the whole, not your best plan, eh, Remi?" Taine felt no guilt in laughing at the idiot sitting beside him in the vehicle. The man held a cold pack to his swollen cheek. "Didn't your parents ever tell you not to poke a wounded beast—they tend to poke back."

"*Freme ta gueule.*"

"You're welcome." Taine always enjoyed pretending he didn't understand French. It amused him to respond incorrectly to being told to shut up. "If you knew your brother-in-law would react badly, why'd you press him so hard?"

"Someone must."

"Next time, bring Caddock." Taine had never enjoyed being dragged into family drama. He had none—and never much saw the point of it. "Back to the inn? It's Monday. I should be heading back to Cardiff. We'll tell them I punched your lights out for insulting my mother."

"You don't know your mother."

"Want to tell them the truth?" Taine shared a smile with the man. "Do you think your brother-in-law will be all right?"

"Hope so. It would break Sarah's heart if he wasn't." Remi reached down to turn the radio up, clearly done with the conversation for the moment.

Can't blame him; bet talking hurts like the devil right now.

The silence on the way back home gave Taine plenty of time to think over the chaotic weekend. He'd expected to have a few drinks, a sore head in the morning, and a good trip down memory lane. He hadn't anticipated Scottie's meltdown or Remi's family angst. The appearance of Graham's nurse had unnerved him as well.

Better not think about him.

Safer.

For both of us.

The new number on his phone mocked him. Taine hadn't stayed at the Fisherman's Refuge for long. Scottie had devolved into worse than insufferable after the attempted attitude intervention, so he'd decided to return to his new home in Cardiff.

Speedy squeaked delightedly once placed in his palatial terrarium. He immediately scurried around to burrow inside his little shire-like cave. Taine found it relaxing to watch him.

"Just you and me, Speedy." He paced the entire length of his home from the front door through the halls, the bedrooms, and finally out into the back garden. He was startled several seconds later when his mobile rang, but smiled at the name on the screen. "Father Wilson."

"Andrew." His adoptive father almost always used his middle name.

The calm, mellow voice with its slight lilt always managed to put him at ease. Taine listened to the old priest's lengthy story about how his weekend had gone. They tended to speak several times a week.

"You're pensive, Andrew." Father Wilson paused in the middle of talking about the upcoming feast day celebration. "Has something happened?"

"Nothing." He hesitated briefly. "I told you about the young nurse who seemed overwhelmed at the hospital a while ago in the cancer ward. I met him again—he's the one who coordinated BC's Graham's care this past year."

"I've prayed for the young man. Offering care to the terminally ill is not an easy choice of work." Father Wilson had sat by many a sickbed, so Taine imagined the man knew what he was talking about. "What about this nurse has you so out of sorts?"

"I'm *not* out of sorts," Taine barked out. He had to chuckle sheepishly. "Perhaps a little off-kilter."

"And?"

And I have no idea.

Taine shrugged, which his adoptive father couldn't see. "He's young."

"As you've mentioned multiple times."

He scratched his still overgrown beard and tried to

determine the best way to rationally explain himself. "He's young."

Well, that's cleared things up, hasn't it?

"Do you like him, Andrew?" Father Wilson had always been a little too intelligent and insightful over the years. It meant Taine had to toe the line more than most teenagers might have. "Or, perhaps you think you might grow to like him if you got to know him?"

"Maybe."

"Taine speech for yes?"

"You've been hosting those classes for teenagers again, haven't you?" He always found it amusing the way the priest tended to pick up certain turns of phrase from his younger parishioners. "How're your knees doing? Still hurting?"

"I'm getting old, Andrew. The joints all start to hurt at this age." Father Wilson sighed. "You weren't called to live a lonely life, lad. If you find this nurse intriguing, what's the harm in talking with him?"

"Are you sure you're a Catholic priest?"

"God judges, son, not I. He gave you to me to cherish and love. What sort of father doesn't love his son, whatever his choices in life?" Father Wilson coughed a few times, having been dealing with a cold for the last week. "I believe it's time for me to rest. Think on it, lad."

When Taine had come out as bisexual, he had fully expected to be at best lectured to constantly. Father Wilson had always been vocal about believing in God's love and mercy. He walked his talk strongly and firmly; he also refused to judge anyone for their actions and decisions.

It had been a moment in his life impossible to forget. Being abandoned as a child had left an indelible mark on his spirit. Taine knew one of the worst flaws in his personality was his habit of keeping people at arm's length and expecting them to disappoint him.

He *expected* abandonment.

Father Wilson hadn't been a perfect adoptive father. No one could claim that distinction. But he had gone above and beyond for a baby left on his doorstep like a bottle of milk.

"Are you feeling any better with your cold? Do you have soup?" Taine worried about being so far from Scotland. It hadn't bothered him until age started to catch up with the priest. He'd even considered moving at least to Glasgow to be within closer driving distance. "Should I come for a visit?"

"You can't run up here every time I have a sniffle." Father Wilson never took his illnesses seriously. "The doctor said I'd be fine in a day or two—it's only a little cold."

They chatted for several more minutes before ending the conversation. Father Wilson's words stayed with Taine. He didn't like Freddie; he hadn't known him long enough to do so as more than a casual acquaintance.

He knew what the real question was.

Do I want to know more?

Standing in his kitchen by the hob, Taine glanced across his empty home. *Alone, no pun intended.* He could admit in the privacy of his mind how lonely he'd been of late. He might not find marriage the least bit attractive, but not having someone to share his life with meant long evenings with no other companion aside from his hamster.

He ate his steak and chips standing by the kitchen sink. No sound in the home to disrupt his thoughts. The silence slowly dissolved his initial intentions to avoid the new name in his mobile.

Do it.

Taine: You awake, Nurse Bunny?

Freddie: It's eight in the evening, of course I'm awake—I'm at work.

Taine: Had dinner yet?

Freddie: I think I had half a curry at some point.

Taine: Half?

Freddie: Shared with one of the doctors. Why?

Taine: Want to have dinner with me?

Freddie: Not tonight, or this week. I'm dealing with several patients including a kid. I'm probably not the best company in the world at the moment.

Taine: Tell me when.

So, not a yes.

And, not a no.

CHAPTER ELEVEN

FREDDIE

The week from hell continued to go downhill rapidly. Freddie split his time between three suddenly terminal patients. His heart ached for all of them—the ones with no hope left. They had nothing to do but wait.

By Friday evening, Freddie had reached a point of sheer exhaustion. He'd driven around Cardiff and the surrounding areas, bouncing from one hospital or facility to the other. Twenty doctors, six specialists, three separate families, all looking at him to organise schedules and manage the whens and wheres of treatment.

Freddie usually found all the chaos to be exhilarating. He loved organising the madness. Helping people get better also made it worthwhile.

Not so much when I can't do a thing to actually make their lives better.

And certainly not this week—maybe next will be better.

Freddie took a moment to rest. He had grown exhausted from watching Katie continue her downhill slide. He wanted to be close enough to help. His stomach grumbled loudly at him, a reminder he'd forgotten to eat both lunch and supper.

The hospital café was already closed. Freddie resigned himself to either another set of leftovers begged from one of the other nurses, or a stale packet from the vending machines. He could head out to his flat, but if he went home now, he'd sleep for hours.

His Mini Cooper had played camper for the past two nights. Freddie didn't know if his back could handle another one. A better question was like how well his brain would function to get him home safely.

"Delivery for a Mr Bunny."

Freddie's head shot up, his eyes suddenly going wide and his brain alert for the first time in hours. He stared dumbfounded at the familiar tall figure of Taine Afoa looming over him in the hallway. "What are you doing here? How'd you even know where to find me? Actually, more importantly, why are you here?"

"You asked the same question twice." Taine apparently didn't see the need to actually answer any of his queries—duplicates or not. He held up a bag in a hand that had sun-warmed bronze skin, which brought to Freddie's mind sandy beaches and island gods. "Hungry? I've brought a chicken curry. It's a favourite of mine from Katiwok."

It had to be the oddest first date on record. They sat side by side in the waiting room in incredibly uncomfortable chairs, sharing a meal from a single container of steamed rice with the curry. They certainly had several of the doctors and nurses giving them odd looks as they walked through to another section of the ward.

Freddie found it unusual and intriguing of the man to simply show up. "I'm appreciative of the meal as I'm half-starved, but it's a bit stalkerish. How'd you know to find me here?"

"I asked BC, who asked Graham, who asked Genevieve."

Freddie blinked at the man. "Never mind."

"Drink?" Taine lifted two bottles of water from the bag. "I've also got chocolate samosas instead of pudding. I think there's a side of spring rolls as well."

"Couldn't wait for me to text you again for a first date?" Freddie lifted the bottle of water to salute him with it. "Thanks for this. It's been a shit week. I'm dead on my feet, and it's not over. This—helped."

"Freddie?" Genevieve paused midstep on her way down the hall. "I thought you went home to rest for a bit?"

"Katie—"

"She'll still be here in the morning, Freddie. Go get a shower and some clean clothes. I don't want to see you until after eight in the morning." She skewered him with a serious glare before her gaze shifted over to Taine. Her eyes gleamed shrewdly at the man. "Could you give him a ride home? I'm worried he'll drive himself into a building in the state he's been in today. Doctor's orders."

"*Gen.*" Freddie tried to sound outraged, but a yawn ruined the effect. "I'm fine to drive."

Taine began putting away the takeaway packets. "Right. You can barely lift a spoon to your mouth."

"Traitor."

Genevieve turned her gaze away from Taine and smirked at Freddie. "You'll thank me later when you're thinking more clearly."

Freddie choked on his last bite of spring roll. "Yes, thanks. *Twmffat.*"

"I heard that, Whittle," she called over her shoulder. "You *will* thank me later—with a bottle of wine. You know the kind."

If Freddie had to be honest, the delicious food had gone straight to his head. It filled him with a beautiful warmth, spreading from his satisfied stomach through his body to make him immediately ready for a nap. Taine being practically pressed up against his side only made the comforting fuzziness worse.

His eyes started to drift close without his permission. "I might could use a nap."

Taine lifted him up out of his chair with embarrassing ease. Freddie struggled out of his hold. He might be sleepy and unsteady, but no first date would be carrying him around like a sack of potatoes.

With his brain not connecting all the dots, Freddie led them to his car instead of following Taine to his. He struggled to keep himself awake while walking. His tripping over his own feet made the man following him chuckle.

Taine's rather impressive hands tightened into fists at his sides. "That's new damage on your car."

"Yes." Freddie had gotten the original words buffed off the door only to have the vandalism repeated for the second time. "They're getting creative."

"They did it again." He sounded as if he spoke through painfully clenched teeth. "What did the police say?"

"What could they say?" Freddie shrugged. "The world will always have its share of bigoted arseholes."

From the deep scowl and murderous glare, Taine didn't feel quite so calm about the situation. He caught Freddie by the shoulder to guide him towards the Bentley a few rows over. The big rugby player didn't say a word while they got into the vehicle.

"How am I supposed to get to work in the morning?" Freddie didn't quite see the point of the fuss being made. "I am perfectly capable of driving myself home."

"No, no you aren't." Taine gestured towards his GPS and Freddie plugged in his address. "Feel free to nap on the way."

Freddie intended to respond. He did. But his eyes wouldn't open, and his mouth wouldn't work.

I can respond later.

Three things occurred to Freddie at the same time when he regained awareness. It was morning. He was tucked into his bed with Bitsy nearby. And someone had left a fairly fresh mug of coffee on his nightstand.

I could've sworn that was a dream.

He found his phone and shoes on the foot of his bed with a note. *Be back to give you a lift. T.* Since the coffee was still warm, he figured Taine couldn't have been gone for too long. He had plenty of time for a shower, breakfast, and deciding how he felt about the man sticking around to ensure everything was fine.

The last one might take me a while.
Coffee first.

CHAPTER TWELVE

TAINE

The last time Taine had slept on a couch had been in the early days of his career. His body had aged significantly since those youthful days of power and flexibility. He'd be aching for a week at this point from a single night on a sofa that had definitely been far too small for his long and muscled self.

What choice did I have?

Once Taine had gotten Freddie settled into bed the night before, he'd been faced with a difficult decision. He couldn't leave and lock the door without taking the keys with him. The young nurse certainly wasn't *awake* or aware enough to voice an opinion on the matter.

A call from Remi at eight in the morning solved his dilemma. The group of men who had decided to stay for a few more days at the inn had decided to come visit him. *Shite.* He'd left Cornwall to allow things to calm down; now the chaos had driven out to see him.

Taine had them bring him coffee and something for Freddie to eat. He set it beside the bed along with a note. The others dragged him away to take the mickey and have breakfast together. The latter was fine; the former would require a great deal of coffee.

Despite his protests, Caddock bullied him into his packed Range Rover. Five former rugby blokes squashed into the SUV looked more like a ton of clowns piling into a tiny car. Elbows were *accidentally* thrown several times before they managed to get situated.

Though the joking around had been mostly lighthearted, a faintly harder edge started to fill the room. Taine exchanged a worried glance with Remi on the return trip to Freddie's flat, where his Bentley was still parked. They both worried about more than half-hearted elbows being thrown about until they all stomped up the stairs together, slightly rowdy and definitely obnoxious, only to find someone already in front of the young nurse's door.

Good news? I no longer want to slam my fist into Scottie's face.

Bad news? All five of us are likely to get arrested for assault.

Two teenage punks stood outside Freddie's flat with aerosol cans of paint in their hands. Taine didn't need to look to his left and right to know he wasn't the only one seething with rage. His arms shook with the effort it took not to immediately pummel the idiots into a mess not even their mums would recognise.

"What. The. Bloody. Hell. Are. You. Doing?" Caddock thankfully stepped out from the group. He was the one most likely to maintain his temper. "I'm waiting for an answer, lads."

"You're…. You're…. Are you Caddock Stanford? The Brute?" One punk's eyes bugged out when he recognised the towering mound of muscles in front of him. His gaze drifted towards the other men crowded by the door. "Holy shite. Look—it's the Frenchie, and BC Brooks, and Tens, and Scottie. What're you doing here?"

Taine stepped up beside his old friend with his arms folded across his chest. He kept them there mostly to ensure he wouldn't give in to the urge to throw a punch—or twenty. "A better question is what you knobdobbers are doing outside Freddie's."

"You know the—"

Taine moved forward, cutting off what would've most certainly been a derogatory word guaranteed to set the lot of them off. He grabbed both idiots by the fronts of their shirts, lifting them off their feet. "Those heroes of yours behind me? BC and the Brute? They're both in relationships with men, who they love with all their hearts. I've dated men and women."

"What?"

Taine shook them hard to shut them up and released them. "I see you around here again. I hear you've been harassing Freddie. I'll ensure your face is suitably rearranged before reporting you to the authorities. Got it? Now fuck off."

They didn't move until Scottie aimed a well-placed kick at their arses. The usually highly vocal man had been oddly silent throughout the brief ordeal. His eyes kept drifting to the partially painted words on the otherwise cheerfully painted blue door.

Maybe he can learn.

"Why do people do shit like this?" Scottie walked over to the edge of the stairwell to ensure the two perpetrators had taken off. "I'm frequently an arsehole, but I'd never do shit like this."

"Well, that's progress, considering you're gay." BC's completely unhelpful comment was met with a glare from Scottie and groans from the others. "What? Am I wrong?"

"No, but yes." Taine swatted him on the back of the head.

"My first wet dream started just like this." Freddie spoke from the now open door. They'd been too focused on the gay-bashing vandals to notice. He glanced over to the fresh paint. "*Coc y gath.* Did you spot them?"

"We handled it," Scottie interjected before anyone else could jump into the conversation—surprising all of them. "Caddock and I are going to buy paint."

"We are?" Caddock stumbled when Scottie grabbed the sleeve of his shirt to drag him towards the stairs. "We apparently are going to buy paint."

Freddie blinked in obvious bewilderment at the retreating backs of the two men. "Did Scottie have a lobotomy? Or a personality transplant since I last saw him?"

"He's a troubled soul." Taine didn't want to get into

Scottie's struggles, so he ignored the snickers from BC. In all honesty, he'd been proud to watch the changes slowly happening in their friend's life. "Did you enjoy your coffee?"

Freddie's eyes flicked from the painted words on his door over to Taine. "Yes? Maybe. Yes."

"Wait a second. Your first wet dream involved us?" Scottie had stopped halfway down the stairs and yelled up to them.

Taine covered his face with his hands. "One step forward, two steps back."

CHAPTER THIRTEEN

FREDDIE

When Monday rolled around again, Freddie felt more exhausted than he had at the start of the weekend. Taine had certainly been a bright spot for him. The additional run-in with the vandals had been more of a dark cloud over his head, dripping rain over him, even if the wall of rugby players had run them off.

Taine had insisted on hanging around for the rest of the weekend. He even came to the hospital, much to the delight of the nurses and patients. Freddie hadn't minded much since the man managed to charm Katie into smiling through her treatments.

For a silent mountain, Taine was surprisingly good with the kids. Not everyone managed to deal with terminally ill children.

It could be an understandably difficult thing to have to face—the mortality of the young. Yet, his new crush managed to be kind and lift their spirits.

Most impressive.

He'd been sad to see Taine leave on Sunday evening. In the short period of time, they'd become accustomed to one another's company. He hoped they'd have dinner again soon.

Mondays could usually be counted on to be as difficult as working at a hospital on the night of a full moon. Today had been more of the same, only worse. Genevieve had refused to stop teasing him about "older rugby players."

Older?

He's not that old, is he?

What a nightmarish day.

The culmination of his Monday had been losing one of his patients. As the coordinator for their care, Freddie generally didn't get physically involved with implementing the treatment. He rarely assisted in operations, and it left him feeling helpless.

Losing a patient when his hands never actively offered healing always tugged at his conscience. Genevieve lectured him on not getting too personally attached. The haunted shadows in her eyes told him she'd been struggling with the same pain.

They all cared. Focusing on oncology wouldn't have been a top choice for any of them if they didn't. Loss came with the territory, yet it hit him hard in the heart each time.

Poor little Katie.

Her family had been utterly devastated. They might've

expected it—a terminal diagnosis came with certain expectations—but knowing wasn't the same as being prepared.

"Freddie?" Genevieve climbed up next to him on the empty bed in the children's ward. She slid her hand into his. "Why don't you take a few days off? Go to London. Or hop on a train to France. My mother would love to see you. Or go somewhere you can eat a ton of cheese."

"My patients—"

"They're well taken care of by the rest of us. You keep your schedules mapped out months in advance." She leaned against him. "One of us needs a holiday, and I've got six operations in the next fortnight, so you're it. Bring me back some rich dark chocolate."

"Of the food or human variety?" Freddie teased. He coughed when she punched him in the side. "What?"

"What happened the last time you tried to help me find a date?" Genevieve asked sardonically.

"Right. Never mind." Freddie cringed at the reminder. The blind date he'd set up for her had ended terribly with food poisoning, crass jokes, and a screaming ex-girlfriend. He'd promised to never do it again. "So, bonbons instead?"

Genevieve eyed him suspiciously. "Are you actually going to take a holiday? One that doesn't involve going to your family farm?"

"You'll nag me to death if I don't." Freddie grunted when her pointy, tawny elbow found his stomach once again. He smiled down at the contrast between their skin tones in their joined hands. "Isn't physical violence breaking the Hippocratic oath? Not sure I want to stay with your parents, though. France is lovely, but not what I need."

"You want cheese."

"Maybe. I might hop on a train to backpack across a few places for the week." Freddie had done something similar before university. His dads had panicked the entire time. "I'll send postcards."

"You could call the rugby man."

"*Gen.*" He glared at her, which had no effect whatsoever. "I'm not calling Taine."

"Fine."

It was his turn to eye her suspiciously. Genevieve had never been known to capitulate quite so easily. He hoped she wouldn't call Taine herself.

"Keep your nose out of my romantic failures, and I'll keep mine out of yours." Freddie tried to nip the issue in the bud.

Won't work, but I might as well try.

Responding like the mature doctor she was, Genevieve shoved him off the bed. They shared a laugh until one of the other nurses poked their head into the room. They quietened down at her glare, but didn't manage to completely muffle their snickers.

"I'll handle the administration stuff for your time off. Wrap up your files and drop them off on my desk." Genevieve hopped off the bed. "We have to take care of each other."

The rest of his evening was spent doing as Genevieve had asked. Freddie left a massive stack of files on her desk. She cursed him all the way out the building.

His awful day continued to improve dramatically when Freddie came home to Bitsy and no new graffiti.

His troublesome neighbours must've feared retribution for their actions. He couldn't imagine why.

Bullies are always cowards in the end.

Thinking about them brought his mind to his upcoming trip and Taine. Should he reach out to the man? They hadn't known each other that long.

It would be weird. Maybe. How else would they get better acquainted? It wouldn't happen by each pretending the other didn't exist.

Freddie could admit to himself he wanted to get to know Taine. The man intrigued him. His rugged looks, deep voice, and incredibly fit body didn't hurt either.

Would Taine want to join him?

More importantly, will he want to get involved with a virgin?

Sitting at the small desk in his flat, Freddie plotted out his plans for a trip to the Netherlands. He'd always wanted to visit some of the famous cheese markets there. He could easily hop on a train—it would be about eight hours, but he'd always been able to sleep while travelling.

He booked his numerous tickets. The train from Cardiff would take him to Paddington. He would go from London to Lille before finally reaching Amsterdam.

The cheese market in Alkmaar would be easily reached from Amsterdam. Freddie had never been to either city. He planned on enjoying his impromptu holiday.

No parents. No patients. No one to stress me out.

I hope.

In his heart, Freddie could admit this was all a distraction.

He ached for the loss of his young patient, the youngest that he'd lost thus far in his career.

Despite her diagnosis, they had all wanted Katie to pull through. She'd been such a bright child. He told himself to remember her light and not sink into depression.

I will help the next one.

I'll do my best to get them through it.

Freddie was reminded of something Graham had repeatedly said during his chemotherapy. He shouted it through tears until he felt a little better. "Fuck cancer."

CHAPTER FOURTEEN

TAINE

At five in the morning, Taine had received a text message from Genevieve. It had a train schedule along with "Pack for a few days." *What*? Freddie had apparently been forced to take a holiday.

What did she expect him to do about it? Taine could admit to finding Freddie attractive. He'd asked the man out on a date and enjoyed it immensely.

Tucking Freddie into his bed, seeing him in the shadow of moonlight, Taine had been faced with how young the nurse was. *Too young for me*. He had to be at least fifteen years older. Wasn't it too much of an age gap?

Do I want to be called a cradle robber?

His dads will likely kill me.

Both Caddock and BC had settled down with men who were significantly younger. Remi's wife Sarah had to be at least ten years his junior. None of them seemed to have struggled with it.

So, why am I?

It's only a holiday, right?

Did he want to do it? Freddie would likely make some assumptions if he showed up, and rightly so. Taine didn't want to give the wrong impression. Another beep from his mobile drew his thoughts away from his indecision.

BC: Get your tanned arse to the train station. Stop dithering.

The gossiping bastard had likely told everyone. Taine didn't have to wait long for confirmation. Multiple messages arrived, all with similar advice: Go to Amsterdam. Have lots of sex. Use protection.

The last two messages had come from Scottie. It surprised him. Not the crassness, but the openness. He appeared to finally be starting to accept himself.

About bloody time.

Now, to travel, or not to travel, that is the question.

Even as he stepped into Cardiff Central station, Taine wondered if this would end up being a massive mistake. He hadn't led a boring life, but he had been known to be cautious. Dating a younger man might come with a massive set of problems.

"Taine?" Freddie stood by a vending machine with a completely shocked expression. "Are you travelling somewhere? Off to Scotland to see your priest?"

"Amsterdam, actually. Though I'm not sure how to feel about Father Wilson sounding like a tawdry port of call." Taine shifted his backpack onto his other shoulder. He waved his train schedule at Freddie. "Several large, noisy birds messaged me at five this morning. You should feel free to tell me to sod off back home."

"Nah. You might as well come along with me." Freddie looked so surprised at his own answer that Taine had to laugh. The nurse joined him a second later. "Nice of them to fob you off on me. Now I won't have to worry about who's going to sit next to me for the seven hours it's going to take to get to Amsterdam. We have four stops. I planned on checking out Lille for a bit before making the last leg of the journey."

"Can I—" Taine started to reach for Freddie's bag, only to get his hand smacked. "Oi."

"I'll carry my own bag.." Freddie peered around him to the train starting to pull up. "Ready to go?"

They were ten minutes into the first leg of their train ride when Taine regretted not splurging for first-class tickets. His immense bulk in both height and muscle didn't compact well into the standard seats. His knee continually pressed against Freddie's leg; their arms brushed against each other constantly.

It would be a rather long trip with a very hard cock. Freddie's scent wafted over him as well. *Not helping.* He smelled of sweet coffee, crisp, clean laundry, and bright citrus.

Their hands kept accidentally touching. Taine would've shoved his into his pockets if it wouldn't have looked odd. Every innocent graze made him ravenous for an intentional one.

Taine bounced his leg, irritated with his own uncharacteristic impatience. "Are we there yet?"

"Problem?" Freddie dropped a hand on his knee, which didn't help Taine's composure at all. "You seem awful jumpy. Are you afraid of traveling like BC?"

"Not quite. BC's afraid of flying, not traveling in general." He was desperate for a distraction from the hand on his leg and latched on to the first thought in his head. "Is young Katie doing better?"

Freddie tensed beside him. He moved his hand and folded both arms across his chest. His eyes turned to stare pointedly out the window at the rapidly passing scenery. "We lost her."

The tone of the three simple words told Taine everything. Freddie sounded lost and desperate to hide it behind a smile. His shoulders had drawn up almost high enough to touch his ears, as if to shield himself from the pain.

Taine couldn't help wondering if Freddie had been forced on this journey by Genevieve. It wouldn't be much of a stretch to worry about the effect losing a child patient could have on anyone in the medical profession. Had she wanted him to go along for the ride to keep an eye on her friend?

He placed a hand tentatively on the younger man's bicep. "I'm sorry for your loss."

"I'm fine. It's fine. She's a client. We can't get attached to all of them. I mean, you couldn't survive working with cancer patients if you become emotionally connected." Freddie turned his head quickly towards Taine with what looked like a forced grin. The smile stretched uncomfortably on his face while his eyes shone with sadness and unshed tears. "Terminal cancer is *terminal* for a reason."

Taine might not have known the caretaker long, but he couldn't stand to see someone suffering so silently. He wrapped his arm around his slender shoulders to pull Freddie as close to him as the seats would allow. "You're not fine. It's shite—cancer is shite. Losing anyone, but particularly a child, would be hard for anyone, whether you're family or her treatment team."

Freddie tried to widen his smile, but it didn't take long for the comforting arm around him to weaken his mask. Taine held him even more tightly when his lips trembled and tears escaped. "I want to save them all. I can't, but I try."

"Of course you do." Taine had seen Father Wilson comfort grieving families many times in his youth. He'd always thought it seemed easy enough. A few Hail Marys, a few Our Fathers, and a kind word; how difficult could it be to make someone feel better? *Very hard.* "I can't imagine how awful this is. I only knew her in passing as a former rugby star going to visit all the kiddies in the cancer ward. Just remember all the joy and smiles you brought to her while doing your best to ease her suffering."

"It's never enough." Freddie sounded so bereft that Taine twisted his head around to brush a kiss against his temple. "Thanks. Losing a patient is the worst part of what I do. It's not a job, not really. I'm more than a nurse."

"You're a caretaker." He shifted in the seat slightly to ease the pain of the arm digging into his side. "You do good work. It's more worthwhile than running a ball up the pitch and careening into the bodies of the opposing team."

Freddie snorted in amusement. It might've been a cross between a laugh and a sob, but neither man commented on it. Taine considered the attempt at a real smile to be a success.

"Do you ever regret deciding to be a nurse?" Taine asked curiously. He didn't think he would've had the strength or dedication to work daily with patients on the brink of death. "Not sure I could do it."

Freddie shrugged, dislodging Taine's arm. "My dads regret it. There are days when I'm not sure I can drag myself to the hospital or a patient's home, but I've never not wanted to be a nurse."

"Not a doctor?"

"Too much stress." Freddie rubbed his arm across his eyes to clear his tears. He offered a slightly less watery grin to Taine. "Want to see what kind of breakfast the onboard café has?"

Taine blinked at the sudden shift of his travel companion's mood. "Breakfast?"

"Coffee. Must have coffee." Freddie scrubbed his eyes again with his sleeve. "Thank you."

They carefully made their way through several train cars to reach the small dining car. It took four cups of coffee for the brightness to return to Freddie's eyes. Taine kept a close watch on him, wanting to help him avoid falling apart in front of others, which clearly bothered the man.

"Here's to fun in Amsterdam. Oh, and good cheese. Lots of dairy gold." Freddie lifted his fifth cup of coffee to offer the toast. "*L'Chaim.*"

"*Sláinte.*"

"Did you just toast me in Gaelic?" Freddie blinked at him.

"Did *you* just toast me in Hebrew?"

"Fair point." Freddie practically inhaled his coffee. "Back to our seats?"

"Back to the loo more likely for you." Taine had only managed one cup to Freddie's five. "Do you normally mainline caffeine?"

"Yes."

"And now I'm understanding why they call you a happy bunny. You're bouncing off the walls from all the coffee and sugar." Taine grunted when Freddie flung an arm into his abdomen. "Truth hurts?"

Freddie walked through one train car before stopping at the end of it and looking around. "*Coc y gath.*"

"Problem?"

"Need the loo."

Taine couldn't help it. He roared so loudly with laughter that an elderly lady shooed them into the next car for disturbing the peace. "Don't piss your pants."

"*Twmffat.*"

CHAPTER FIFTEEN

FREDDIE

Five cups of coffee had been a distraction to stop himself from thinking about kissing. A fatal flaw in his plan came from spending the next hour or so of the trip to Paddington Station going back and forth to the loo. Taine kindly didn't smirk at him, at least not where he could see it.

Lips had never been an obsession of Freddie's; he tended to be more of an abdomen and leg person. The taut muscles on a man could always twist his stomach into knots. It certainly explained why he'd always enjoyed watching football and rugby—players tended to have impressively muscled legs.

Taine's lips, though.

Freddie's eyes would drift down to the man's mouth anytime he spoke. It had gotten to the point of being more than a little embarrassing. He couldn't help himself; the man's lips were full and plumper than they had a right to be. His own felt thin and small by comparison.

But Taine's….

Hell. Stop staring.

Trying to force his mind to focus on something else, Freddie's gaze roamed down towards one of the many black-and-grey tattoos on Taine. Visualising them didn't do much help to re-centre himself when his brain immediately latched on the idea of where else the skin might be inked. *Not. Helpful.*

"They're *moko.*" Taine's deep voice broke into his self-recriminations. He gestured to the band inked on his forearm, visible with his shirtsleeves shoved up. "This is called *ahu ahu matoroa.* It's meant to signify talent in sport, amongst other things. I've turtles along my spine and one on my shoulder, another traditional style. I've also got my left leg and my shoulders covered in a more modern twist of the typical Maori ink. It's my way of paying homage to a part of my family's ancestry. Do you have any tattoos?"

"Aside from the one on my right wrist that you've already seen?" Freddie pulled up his sleeve to reveal a second *Doctor Who* quote slightly further up his right forearm. "'We're all stories in the end.' I have the Hogwarts crest on my left leg in watercolour, a nurse's symbol with wings on my back, and one of the tailor of Gloucester from the Beatrix Potter story on my left arm. I might get a new one on my chest."

"Of what?" Taine continued his perusal of the small mouse tattooed on Freddie's left arm.

"Cheese."

Taine practically gawked at his answer. "Cheese?"

"I'm a fan," Freddie asserted defensively. "What's wrong with cheese?"

"Nothing." Taine seemed to shift from surprise to amusement quickly. "Do you have a dairy fetish?"

"Aren't you *hilarious*." Freddie chose to ignore the question. He grabbed his itinerary from the front pocket of his backpack. "We've a bit of a wait once we get to St Pancras in London before we catch the Eurostar train to Lille. Want to explore around the station a little when we get there?"

His not-so-subtle ploy to derail the conversation worked for the moment. They used their phones to hunt for a few places in London to visit while killing time before their third train departed. His excitement started to build at getting away from everything for a week—the attractive man next to him would be the cherry on top of his Bakewell tart.

The British Library near the station appealed the most to Freddie. Taine didn't seem to mind. He'd been to London before, so it appeared more important to him that Freddie enjoyed himself.

"Are you going to continue to stare at my lips whenever you look my direction?" Taine's voice dropped down to a husky whisper. "If you are, why don't you bring yours a little closer to mine? You'll see them far better with your mouth than your eyes."

Cursing his exuberant and generally impulsive nature, Freddie leaned forward until their lips hovered a breath away from each other. One strong exhale could bring them close enough to qualify as a kiss. Taine didn't move backwards or forwards; they both waited for the deadlock to be broken.

"Oh, why not," Freddie muttered impatiently. He surged forward, closing the distance. His lips smacked awkwardly to the left of Taine's, which caused the man to chuckle. "Oh, *coc y gath,* sorry."

"Calm down." Taine caught Freddie's chin in his hand and guided him closer. His mouth controlled the connection. They had to tilt to avoid their noses mashing uncomfortably. The former rugby player's tongue darted across Freddie's lips and pressed the advantage. He delved expertly into their true first touch. "Now *that* is a kiss."

"You should be ashamed."

Freddie jerked away from Taine and snapped around to find a woman in her sixties glaring at them—or at Taine specifically. "Pardon?"

"You should be ashamed." She pointed a bony finger at Taine. "Corrupting a young teenager. Is that legal? I've half a mind to report you. Are you okay, young man? Did he force you away from your parents?"

"A teenager?" Freddie swallowed down an irrational burble of laughter. "I'm twenty-six years old."

"Oh. *Oh, dear.* I'm so sorry." She covered her mouth in obvious embarrassment. "You look so young. I just assumed. Carry on then, loves. Never you mind me. It's always good to see someone enjoying the pleasures of life."

The two men stayed silent after accepting her apology. Freddie only dared to peek at Taine out of the corner of his eye once the woman had gone back to her seat. *A clear mistake.* It started with a snort, muffled quickly by his hand, but quickly dissolved into laughter anyway; it continued until their sides ached and they were gasping for air.

Freddie regained his composure just as the train pulled into Paddington station, forcing him to shelve any comments about the kiss. "Ready for the next stage of the journey?"

They caught the train to St Pancras. After perusing the library, they hopped on their third train of the day, the one that would take them to Lille. His excitement continued to build. The passing scenery only made it all the more thrilling for him.

"About earlier." Taine brought him back to the humorous moment when they'd been kissing, only he didn't seem amused. "I am too old for you. She won't be the first person to make assumptions."

Freddie waited until a group of passengers had walked past their seats on the way through to voice his opinion. "Too old? On what planet? I spend my days dealing with things most would find too hard to even comprehend. Guys my age? They never manage to deal with it. I might be a 'happy bunny,' but I've no time for silly nonsense. I've suddenly developed a thing for older men."

"Really? Suddenly?"

"Apparently." Freddie couldn't help caving to the urge to lust after those lips again. "It's a new thing, maybe it's you specifically. Older certainly seems better."

"Me?"

Freddie brought his hand up, dragging his thumb across Taine's lower lip, grinning at the way the man's facial hair tickled his finger. His laugh disappeared into a groan that he barely managed to swallow when Taine flicked his tongue across the teasing digit. "Definitely a you phenomenon."

"Is it?" Taine caught Freddie's wrist with his rough, calloused fingers. "We'll see."

CHAPTER SIXTEEN

TAINE

Freddie had tasted of sugar, coffee, and a hint of mint. Taine couldn't shake the flavour. He wanted another kiss.

The hour in London, the time in Lille, none of it really registered to him. Taine could only think about stripping Freddie down to nothing. He started to hunger for it— something he hadn't felt in his core for a while.

While Freddie might not have a rugby-sized body, the young nurse looked fit. *Very fit.* He reminded Taine of some of the slight fishermen in Scotland. They might be slender, but their muscles were hard as iron.

My first crush.

He could still remember with a visceral cringe trudging into confession with tears in his eyes. Father Wilson hadn't condemned him to hell. The priest had rather controversially told him God had more important sins to worry about than a young man's wandering eye.

In his youth, Taine hadn't quite understood how progressive his adoptive father actually was at the time. As an adult, he had massive amounts of respect for the man who refused to be cowed by his cowl. Father Wilson could've easily condemned him at a young age, sent him off to an institution. It had happened to other children and teenagers.

The fate of one of his close friends in school still haunted him even now. Taine had dedicated much of his charitable work outside of the hospital to the rights and protections for other LGBT youth. He fully believed someone had to offer them help when their families abandoned them.

"You've gone all serious." Freddie looked at him over the top of what appeared to be a well-read copy of *The Lion, The Witch, and The Wardrobe*. The cover had started to warp at the corners, and the colours had faded. "Something wrong?"

Taine shook his head to answer and clear his mind. "Thinking about an old friend."

"A first crush?"

"Not quite." Taine nudged Freddie with his elbow. "How long until we reach Amsterdam?"

"Thirty minutes? Depends on if there are any delays." He lifted the novel to begin reading again. "I have other novels if you want to borrow one."

"Now you offer?" Taine tilted his head to the side with a wry grin. "How far into our journey are we, and you're just offering to share your entertainment?"

"I couldn't decide if you were worthy of handing over one of my treasures." Freddie chuckled, though it was hidden by the aged pages. "Still not 100 percent convinced."

"Treasures?" He tapped his finger against the flaking edges of what had been a beautiful cover of the C.S. Lewis paperback. "Not sure this qualifies."

"It's given me hours upon hours of joy. The words within have carried me to faraway magical places that only exist in the written word." Freddie closed the book and held it loosely in his hands. "I could travel across the universe for a few quid at a used bookstore. Seems like quite the treasure to me."

"I stand corrected." Taine had never been much of a reader. He'd always preferred either being outdoors or watching the telly. "Never heard anyone speak so eloquently on the topic of reading—particularly when waving around a copy of a children's book."

"Have you read it?"

"Saw the movie."

"You *saw* the film?" Freddie scoffed at him. He pulled the ticket stub out of his novel and flipped to the first page. "Well, pull your mind out of the clouds, I'll read it to you."

"On the train?" Taine glanced around at the other passengers. "Not sure we should have story time now."

"What better time?" His deep brown eyes followed Taine's lighter ones to take a peek at everyone. "Maybe it'll teach them something as well."

"We've only got thirty minutes." Taine didn't mind as such if Freddie wanted to read to him. He was far more entertained by the way those eyes brightened in irate fury. "Maybe you can tuck me in tonight with a story?"

Tuck me in with something.

Freddie whacked him on the arm with his book. "*Honestly.*"

"Is that a yes or a no?"

"You'll have to be a good boy and listen to the story to find out." He gave Taine a boyish grin. "Can you be a good boy?"

"Not sure I fit into that category." Taine let his eyes drift lingeringly and longingly down Freddie's body. "You, on the other hand, definitely could."

He swatted Taine on the arm for the second time. "What would your Father Wilson say about it?"

"Confession is good for the soul." He actually thought the priest would like Freddie and likely call the nurse one of God's kind hearts. "Why *The Lion, The Witch, and The Wardrobe*?"

Freddie's gaze dropped to the book in his hands before turning it towards Taine to stare intensely at him. "You should always start an adventure at the beginning. You never know what you'll miss by trying to race ahead to the climax."

"One should never rush a climax." Taine blocked the third whack to his arm. "Well? Let's start with the foreplay—I mean reading."

"You'll have people yelling at us for being degenerates again." Freddie sounded more amused than concerned. "I've never been scolded on a train by a stranger."

They didn't manage much beyond the first chapter before the train pulled into the station in Amsterdam. A couple of children who had been sitting two rows behind them came up to listen to the tale. Their parents, thankfully, didn't shout at them for corrupting the youth, so they considered it a win.

Then again, if he'd been travelling with two small children, any port in a storm would do for a distraction to keep them from nattering on about "are we there yet?"

The Alkmaar Cheese Market was an easy distance from the hostel Freddie had picked to stay in. Taine took one look at all the backpackers loitering in the lobby and made an easy, quick decision. He grabbed the nurse by the hand and led him out of the place.

Not a chance am I sleeping with those rowdy teenagers. I'm way beyond the age of crashing on bunk beds for the night while sharing a room with a group of high-off-their-noggins kids who are barely out of their teens by the looks of it. Not a bloody chance.

"Will you stop dragging me along like a wayward toddler?" Freddie stumbled a few times before finding his feet. He glared, looking more like an angry kitten than anything else, and Taine had to turn his head to hide his smirk. "Why are we leaving? I got on my mobile earlier to book an extra bed so we'd both have somewhere to sleep. I made reservations."

"There's not enough bleach in the entire city to entice me to sleep on those sheets." Taine had never considered himself to be overly fussy, but the older he got, the more he appreciated comfort and convenience over cost-effectiveness. He'd gone beyond being able to sleep on lumpy mattresses. It was difficult not to see it as yet another glaring example of the differences in their ages. "I've a better idea."

While Freddie peppered him with questions, Taine sent a text to Remi to see if Sarah knew anyone in Amsterdam. She didn't. Thankfully, Scottie, of all people, did have a mate whose sister ran the Seven Bridges Hotel, an old canal house in one of the most beautiful districts in the older part of the city.

One taxi ride later saw them standing in front of the boutique hotel. It hopefully smelled less like a university flat full of stinky blokes than the hostel had. Taine had asked for either rooms that were connected or across the hall from one other.

I'll have that bedtime story.

Or maybe, I'll write one of my own.

After all, it occurred to him that not every story had to be written down on paper with ink. Theirs could easily be etched into their skin using the bed for a desk. They could provide the canvas and paints with their body.

Taine had his doubts, even on the cusp of seducing Freddie into his bed. Age differences made relationships—or even casual sex—complex. He disliked complications.

Life since rugby had been about removing complications from his life. His cock appeared to be guiding him right into the middle of one. *Do I mind? Does it matter to me what others might say?*

After all, me and Freddie? We might be a story to remember.

CHAPTER SEVENTEEN

FREDDIE

How did this happen?

One moment Freddie had been safely set to sleep at the hostel, only to end up in a slightly swanky hotel across the city. He'd *never* stayed in a boutique hotel before and certainly not with a staggeringly attractive man across the hall from him. The rooms were filled with interesting antiques that would've made Francis drool; he'd been sure to snap a few photos to text to the interior decorator, who specialised in restoring vintage furniture.

Supper had been thankfully neither swanky nor posh. They'd found a great little café not far from the hotel to start their evening with *stamppot*. He'd always wanted to try the Dutch version of bubble and squeak, and it didn't disappoint.

Taine had required two bowls of the sausage, mashed potatoes, and sauerkraut. He'd still appeared hungry afterwards. They'd walked around the streets until they'd found a bar that served not only a wide selection of beers but had a cheese plate as well.

They managed to explore all around the hotel, stopping in at various pubs for a pint—or two. A few drinks had done wonders for Freddie's courage. It had also made him astonishingly randy, not a brilliant thing with the handsome man at his side.

It's the beer's fault. That's what did this.

Alcohol lowering his inhibitions certainly explained why he now sat on the bed in Taine's room, reading from the Narnia Chronicles. They'd made it to chapter five. They had to stop and drunkenly giggle frequently as his captive audience of one insisted on making a running commentary on the story.

Edmund's a bit of a tosser, isn't he? Do you think C.S. Lewis had eaten a few special Amsterdam brownies before he wrote this? What idiot child goes to a stranger's house for tea?

The continuous commentary had them both rolling around on the bed in fits of laughter. Freddie had to wipe tears from his eyes; they both gasped for air. In the midst of the hilarity, he somehow wound up with his hand on a rather large, hard thigh that definitely wasn't his own.

His breath hitched for a far different reason than humour. He couldn't resist flexing his fingers, digging them in a little to test the taut muscles. Taine's eyes had gone an almost molten metal colour; it was like peering into a vat of gold.

He couldn't help thinking Taine looked exactly like a lion preparing to pounce on his prey; Aslan had clearly sunk into his subconscious. Freddie hadn't ever had a man appear so riveted by him. It lit a furnace in his body, and it definitely wasn't the beer talking.

From raucous amusement to a heady silence, Freddie lay in the bed next to the man, his hand on Taine's leg the only physical connection between them. He kept his eyes focused on his fingers—not Taine's eyes. It felt as if he were fighting a magnetic force to avoid them.

What's the worst that can happen if our eyes meet in this heated moment?

Sex?

Was he ready to lose his virginity? He hadn't exactly been waiting for Mr Perfect. It had been more of not wanting to make a mistake with his first adventure in intercourse.

God, I sound like a damn school nurse giving a presentation on sex.

"Frederick?" Taine's fingers wrapped around the back of his neck to guide him up the bed. He shimmied up the mattress until they were nose to nose. "In your packing, did you think to bring condoms? I did, but I always like to know there's extras hanging around."

Freddie didn't know whether to respond to the use of his full name or the question about condoms. He went for blunt honesty. "Condoms aren't generally high on the packing lists of virgins, not when intending to travel alone."

"Virgins?" Taine's hand drew him closer until their noses actually touched. "You've never had sex, at all?"

"Not all sex is intercourse." He offered a wry smile to the obviously surprised man. "Something wrong with being a virgin?"

Taine canted his head slightly, causing their noses to brush together. "How many beers did you have tonight?"

"No idea. Too many to count, but not enough I can't speak in full sentences." Freddie didn't think his mind had gone completely muddled with the alcohol. He made the mistake of dropping his eyes down to those lips that had drawn him in every time they'd seen each other. He leaned in until they almost kissed. "What's it matter?"

"It does." Taine closed the distance, a soft and gentle caress of their lips. "Why don't you read some more?"

"Read?" Freddie ran his fingers from Taine's jaw along his chin up to his mouth. "Maybe there's a story in Braille written on your skin."

He grabbed Freddie by the wrist to pull his hand away. "Oh, you are a temptation, but I'd rather we were both sober for your first time."

He's confident.

The journey, the beer, and the early morning caught up to Freddie from one moment to the next. His hand dropped to the mattress while he dropped onto his back. He couldn't keep his eyes open as his head hit the pillow.

Freddie awoke the next morning in a room that wasn't his own. Taine had clearly already gotten up, showered, and had time to grab a cup of coffee. He sat on a chair across from the bed; a mug of what smelled like strong coffee rested on the nightstand within easy reach.

Am I drooling over the caffeine or the shirtless man in the room?

He'd never been one to awkwardly avoid uncomfortable topics of conversation. It came from his work; having to handle the telling of bad news to already fragile people had toughened him up in some ways. He found being direct usually worked best. "Did you not want to shag me?"

Maybe that was too direct?

Taine spluttered coffee across his bare chest, making Freddie feel as if he could have the best of both worlds. *Would it be too forward to lick it off him?* "I definitely did 'want to shag' you."

"Well? What happened?"

"People put so much pressure on their first time. It's not some mystical experience." Taine brushed coffee off his bare skin, and Freddie found himself riveted to the movements. "First, fiftieth, or last, you should always be sober enough to not only enjoy it, but more importantly, consent."

"Sober? We weren't completely pissed." Freddie had been aware enough to read *The Lion, The Witch, and The Wardrobe.* "I could've managed it."

"We were giggling like a pair of hyenas at the zoo." Taine shifted forward in the chair and rested his elbows on his thighs. "Maybe I want you cognisant enough to know who you're screaming 'yes' to through the night and into the morning. You'll probably throw my name in there a few times."

"Will I?" Freddie shoved the blankets away, suddenly overly warm in the cool hotel, and thanked God that he'd thought to bring his backpack over from his room. He hopped smoothly out of bed and hoped the loose pyjama bottoms covered his morning wood. "You sound like one of my aunt's telly shows, all attractively seductive drama with no satisfaction because it's fantasy, not reality."

"Good sex, Frederick, is not about fantasy versus reality." Taine stood up to his impressive six-foot-five height and stalked over to where Freddie had started to hunt for his clothes for the day. The larger man's hand drifted across his pyjama-covered arse to settle comfortably there. "The best sexual encounters blend the two together until your mind abandons logic to pleasure."

"Is it? What else is sex?" Freddie didn't have a clue how he managed to keep his voice steady with those fingers splayed across his arse. One thumb casually dipped along the seam of his pyjamas to press slightly into the crease. "I imagine you're only too happy to tell me all about it."

The truth of the matter was, Freddie had no idea what to do next. He'd been bent over to go through his backpack when Taine grabbed him. Should he stand up again? Would it be better or worse?

"What is sex?" Taine's fingers skimmed along his spine to catch him by the shoulders to guide him to an upright position. "Have you ever looked through a kaleidoscope? Sex is looking through one of those while on an acid trip. It's enjoying a night of drinking and having the perfect fry-up in the early hours of the morning. Decadent. Greasy. Feels as if it's terrible for you, but so miraculous you'll risk the fire to gobble it all up. It's craving chocolate only to have someone gift you with enough of the best treats to binge on for days."

"I might not have been buggered before, but I've had sexual encounters. It's never been all of that." Freddie had enjoyed most of what he'd done previously. He couldn't help wondering if maybe his—or his partner's—skills hadn't been what they should. "It's never been half of that."

Taine began walking, forcing Freddie backwards until his legs bumped into the table that ran along one of the walls. His hands came up to rest against the wall, bracketing the smaller man between his arms. "You haven't done it right, Frederick, not even close."

"Haven't I?" Freddie didn't know what to do with his hands, so he went with what soothed his growing arousal. He planted them on Taine's sides, his fingers touching the smooth, tawny skin. They were so close that the former rugby player's chest hairs brushed against him. "Are you going to teach me? Should I wear short trousers and knee-high socks? Play the student to your teacher?"

Taine swallowed with such difficulty that Freddie heard it loudly. "Definitely more of the fantasy—maybe not the first time. You never know, you might enjoy a wooden ruler across your arse."

It was Freddie's turn to gulp when Taine squeezed a hand between the table and his body to swat him on the arse. *Goodness.* He hadn't expected it.

Or expected to like it. Do I like it? Maybe he should do it again. Coc y gath. *I better be on my way to my first time. I'm harder than a block of cheddar.*

Taine leaned into him further, demonstrating quite blatantly that it was a *shared* problem. "Oh, *oh,* I see. Frederick, you have untapped depths to explore, don't you?"

"If you don't stop saying my name like that, I'm going to have issues whenever someone uses my full name. I'm not one of Pavlov's dogs to be trained to harden when I hear it." He winced at giving away some pertinent information. Taine didn't really need to know how arousing his voice could be. The man probably already knew the effect he had on others— or on him, at least. "Just *quit* it."

"Something wrong with the way I say *Frederick?*" Taine nipped at the tip of Freddie's nose. He turned his head to brush his lips against the younger man's ear and murmur repeatedly, "*Frederick. Frederick. Frederick.*"

"I can't decide if you're trying to desensitise me or break my cock." Freddie couldn't figure a way to subtly reach down and adjust himself without rubbing all over both of their shafts. "This isn't going to be a repeat of last night, is it? It's brilliant to know chivalry isn't dead—Aunt Anna will be beyond thrilled. I'd be happier to be on the other side of virginland."

Taine eased his head back to smirk at him. "Am I making you nervous, Frederick? You chatter a bit when you're nervous."

"My thirsty ferret is harder than a block of cheddar," Freddie retorted sharply.

"Your thirsty ferret?"

"Welsh thing."

"Thirsty. Ferret." Taine sounded out the words slowly in obvious disbelief.

"What? Don't you Scots have weird terms for your cocks?"

Freddie felt his heart start to race when the private parts in question nudged against one another. "Not even one?"

"I did once hear someone call it a satter spatterer."

Freddie had no idea how Taine managed to say "satter spatterer" without even a hint of amusement. "And you have a problem with my words?"

Taine bumped up against him with a wicked smile twisting his lips upward. "I don't care what you call your cock—soon you won't be capable of much beyond asking for more."

CHAPTER EIGHTEEN

TAINE

Of his partners over the years, Taine couldn't recall ever being someone's first. He barely remembered his own. The sex had been awkward and certainly better the second time around.

He'd meant what he'd said to Freddie. Going from virgin to not wouldn't be earth-shattering, but the sex itself could be when done right. They'd write a bestseller between them on the luxurious sheets—maybe in the shower and on the couch. *Wall might be brilliant as well.*

I've never been much of a reader—this might change my mind.

And now, I put words into action.

He hadn't gotten a ton of sleep through the night. His thoughts had been filled with deflowering his first innocent—

not that Freddie actually qualified as one.

Who came up with that term? Deflowering? It sounds like something Father Wilson does in his garden.

In his thirties, Taine had gained an appreciation for all the toys and decadence that came with sex done right. He wished he'd brought more of his arsenal than lube and condoms. Freddie might enjoy a bit of a prologue before the main thrust of the story.

Freddie stepped out of the en-suite a few seconds later. He'd ducked into the shower, claiming he didn't want his first time to involve bad breath or anything unsanitary. Taine had told him to be more concerned about morning wood.

For having hopped in the bath, Freddie had returned to the room wearing pyjama bottoms. Clothing was usually optional in bed. Taine, however, didn't want to immediately jump to naked, so he didn't mind.

Staying on the edge of the mattress, Taine watched Freddie run a towel roughly through his short brown hair. He planned on taking his time, indulging all of his desires in the lithe body standing before him. The only thing left to determine was where to begin.

He thanked his lucky stars that he'd opted for the room with a king-sized bed. It would certainly come in handy. But first, he wanted another kiss—or twenty.

He strode across the room until they once again stood toe to toe, but not quite nose to nose. Freddie stood quite a bit shorter, something that might make for interesting positions. *Later, Taine, later. Let's not scare him on his first round of rumpy-pumpy.*

A fascinating aspect of Freddie's personality came to light almost immediately. He had not a shy or coy bone in his body, but a massive amount of impatience. The lithe man grabbed a handful of Taine's hair to yank him close enough for him to crush their lips together.

Their moment was momentarily interrupted by a jazzy ring from Taine's mobile, which he ignored. Freddie's went off a second later. The nurse grabbed for it, likely worried it might be a client or doctor. He gave a breathy "Hello?" only to toss the phone over to Taine.

"Yes?" Taine's eyebrows lifted, only to immediately drop when he scowled at BC's cheerful greeting. "I'm busy. Is this important?"

"Yes." BC sounded more excited than the time he'd scored a try in a critical match. "About the Sin Bin."

"Are you serious?" Taine glared at Freddie's mobile, wishing he could reach through it to whack his friend across the head. "What about it? The workshop is a terrible idea."

"I know, got a better one." BC paused for a moment, likely for dramatic effect. "A nightclub—a gay nightclub."

"What?" Taine had to think to get the question out when Freddie tentatively reached out to trace one of his tattoos with a gentle finger. "In Cornwall?"

"No, in Cardiff. It'll be brilliant. A rugby-themed nightclub. We can have matches playing on screens. Scottie can run it." BC's idea had started off brilliant and veered off into insanity at the end.

"Scottie? You want the one member of our group in dire need of anger management to run a nightclub. Can you imagine him dealing with customers? He'd end up with assault charges in less than an hour of opening." Taine restrained himself from flinging the phone across the room. He wanted to be ripping Freddie apart sexually and not tearing a strip off his old friend for interrupting him. "Have you taken leave of your senses?"

"You'll be there. Remi's promised to help. Caddock knows about running a pub. It's brilliant. Doesn't the Sin Bin scream nightclub? Come in with us. It can be a partnership between the five of us." His voice turned to pleading quickly. "Please?"

"If I say yes, do you promise not to call again—or gossip with the others about my being busy on holiday?" Taine had no doubts they'd all be taking the mickey soon enough for his dalliance with Freddie.

"Not a chance, but you'll do it anyway." BC chuckled.

"*Bollocks.*"

"I'll take that as a yes. Don't forget to use a condom." BC hung up before he could respond.

Shite.

"Where were we?" Taine tossed the phone casually to a nearby chair and returned to the man in front of him. "Oh, yes."

For all his earlier almost incessant chatter, Freddie quietened quickly. *I suppose it's hard to natter on with my mouth on his.* Their silky tongues taunted one another, darting in and out of open mouths.

Taine reached out to grip the table behind Freddie for support. A bad decision, as it turned out, when their cocks brushed together and the wood creaked dangerously under the pressure of his fingers. He released the edge of the antique to avoid actually cracking it.

Does travel insurance cover accidents caused in the midst of a sexual fever?

Dropping his hands heavily on Freddie's shoulders, Taine walked backwards towards the bed, bringing his soon-to-be lover with him. He stopped when his legs bumped against the mattress. There'd been enough kissing for now.

Time to start the ascent to the pinnacle of pleasure.

Hope the walls are soundproof.

Hope to hell I brought enough lube.

Two critical things Taine discovered during his first experience had always stuck with him. Always use enough lube. Always take your time. He'd never rush good sex unless it was in public. Public indecency was never a good idea—if you got caught.

Blithering, idiotic knobdobber.

He exchanged places with Freddie, pushing him down to sit on the edge of the mattress. "Sober? Breath fine? Consenting?"

"Yes, yes, and yes."

"Remember that I expect you to be screaming it in a bit," Taine repeated his words from the night before with a smirk. "You could've left the pyjamas on the bathroom floor."

Kneeling down on the expensive-looking rug, Taine placed his hands firmly on Freddie's knees. He earned a snicker when he slowly spread his legs. It took no effort at all to yank the blue-striped pyjamas off the man and discard them over his shoulder.

"You left your boxers, but kept the trousers?"

Freddie quirked his lips up into a boyish grin. "Surprise."

The humorous mood dropped away with the edging of his hands along the inside of Freddie's thighs. Taine bent his head to lave his tongue along the sensitive skin his fingers had trailed over. Freddie shifted on the bed, and his cock twitched with each inch of leg crossed.

He avoided the rigid shaft all but begging him for attention. His fingers dipped down to tease the heavy sac underneath it. Freddie arched up slightly off the bed.

When his lips finally moved to feather over the head of his cock, Freddie's fingers dug into the mattress behind him. His legs tensed while Taine licked and sucked the first inch of his shaft. He planned on bringing the younger man to his first climax to ensure they could take their time with the rest.

Despite his obvious attempts to restrain himself, Taine worked Freddie up to an initial satisfying explosion. He didn't wait for him to regain his footing. His hands grabbed the lithe man to shove him further up on the bed.

Taine pulled off his own pyjama bottoms and shorts, kicking them to the side easily and straddling Freddie on the bed. He deflected the hand reaching towards the hardness between his legs. "This isn't about me, Frederick. Not this time."

With his hands resting on Freddie's sides, Taine licked down his neck and across his collarbone to tongue one pebble-hard nipple and then the other. His teeth worried one of them, tugging on it, not to the point of pain, earning a series of low moans from the man writhing underneath him.

"Gods above." Freddie looped his arms around Taine's

broad back. He arched up into the taunting mouth, throwing his head back into the pillow. "*Yes.*"

Taine smiled against the pale olive skin underneath his lips, unable to help a bit of gloating. "Told you."

"*Twmffat.*"

Tweaking one of the over-sensitised nipples, Taine began his journey south while his fingers continued to explore Freddie's chest. They roamed across the lightly muscled abdomen.

Taine wrapped his hand around Freddie's shaft, which had already grown hard once again under his lengthy ministrations. He tugged on it. It twitched with each shake.

Nudging his knee between the smaller man's legs, Taine stretched out between them. It gave him the perfect view of the lovely, long but lean shaft and heavy balls. His gaze drifted lower to the pert cheeks waiting for him to part them.

He nuzzled and mouthed at the length of Freddie. Grabbing the lube from the bed where he'd tossed it, Taine covered the slenderest of his fingers. He circled the tightness and delved casually in up to the top of his fingernail.

Distracting the trembling man with his tongue, Taine worked his finger in with the lube. He added a second once he met no resistance. The slight stretch caused his cock to pulse where it was pressed against Freddie's leg.

The addition of a third digit caused Freddie's breath to audibly hitch. Taine waited patiently for him to buck slightly before continuing the shallow probing. They moved deeper in until the tip of his index finger nudged against the sensitive bud, causing an immediate reaction from the man at his mercy.

He didn't have to be a mind reader to know Freddie had more than reached a stage of complete eagerness. It didn't hurt to make certain, though, did it? He continued spreading and twisting his fingers, earning all sorts of sounds.

Taine slid back up to align their bodies better. His fingers gripped Freddie's hair to hold him still while his other hand grasped him by the neck. Their mouths met in a painfully crushing kiss.

The hand on Freddie's neck made way for his lips. He bit, licked, and sucked on the tender flesh until his mark had been left, rubbing his beard across it to tease out another moan. They were as ready as they were going to be.

Rolling his hips from side to side, Taine bumped their staffs together. Freddie tried to shift up slightly to better align their bodies, but his muscled bulk held him still. From the groans and sharp hisses, his nurse had gone from aroused to aching for it.

"Are you ready then?" Taine reached between them to guide his cock. He waited for the impatient nod to continue. "Good. Not sure I could've waited much longer."

"You?" Freddie managed to spit out while his breath continued to come in hard gasps. "I'm dying."

"Not yet, you aren't." Taine paused to grab a condom. He slid it on with exaggerated slowness to aggravate Freddie, who narrowed his eyes. "Let me add a bit more lube."

With a fixed, unhurried push, Taine eased himself into the well-lubed and prepared arse. He'd wanted the closeness of being chest to chest for their first time. *Next time, next time I'll position us so I can get my hands on that pert bottom.*

His hand itched to get a good swat or two in to encourage Freddie to meet his thrusts.

Slow and steady won the race, however, as Freddie groaned in satisfaction with him. They stayed connected without moving for what felt like a century to Taine. He wanted the smaller man to be truly adjusted to his sizeable length before he ground him into the bed.

"Move, you obstinate bastard." Freddie lifted his hips up as much as the heavy weight on him would allow. "*Coc y gath.* I want more—need more."

Happy to provide what had been begged of him, Taine planted his hands on either side of Freddie for leverage to slowly grind into him. He caught the man's earlobe between his teeth, worrying it while amping up the strength of his thrusts.

When it felt like they'd toed too close to the final line, Taine eased up on the pace. He slowly rolled his hips to match their languid kiss. He tortured them both with the agonising speed that edged them on the precipice of completion.

It proved to be a double-edged sword. His body ached for completion, as well. Taine dropped down until his chest rubbed against Freddie's.

Reaching between their bodies, his fingers wrapped around Freddie's already leaking shaft. Taine ploughed into the man while his hand stroked at an equally manic speed. He angled to continually bash against the bundle of nerves guaranteed to make it brilliant for the man underneath him. His hope was to make this a first time to remember.

I want him to think about this whenever he's hard.

I want him to long for me.

Beg for me.

He brought his partner to what he hoped was a mind-blowing climax—the tightening around his own cock sent him tumbling into his own whirlwind of pleasure. It left them both choking for air. He dropped his head against Freddie's sweaty chest, completely exhausted from the exertion.

Taine collapsed on his back next to the heavily breathing Freddie. He could barely manage the effort to discard the used condom. "How's it feel?"

"What? Not being a virgin?" Freddie managed between laboured pants. "Exhausting and sodding brilliant."

"Well, technically, you're still one." Taine grabbed the edge of the sheet to wipe sweat from his brow.

"How'd you figure that?" Freddie twisted over on his side to glare at him. "I believe I'm not gone enough to have forgotten your todger pressed up into me."

"You've been 'pressed,' but have you done the pressing?" Taine reached over to grab the previously discarded bottle of lube and tossed it at him. "Want me to bend over for you?"

"*What?*" Freddie sounded so surprised that Taine lifted his head up to get a closer look. "Are you serious?"

"Why wouldn't I be?"

"You don't—" Freddie didn't seem to know how to complete the sentence.

Taine decided to offer him a way out of the suddenly and amusingly awkward moment. "Don't you want to say you've buggered the massive rugby star?"

While, generally speaking, Taine preferred to be a top in

bed, he'd never been one of those men who shied away from being on the bottom. Sex was sex—good sex was like a game-winning try during the last seconds of a championship match.

And Freddie?

Freddie was definitely good sex. Taine didn't know how things would play out with the younger man. It could just be a holiday fuck and nothing more—it wouldn't be the first time.

"I think you've broken me." Freddie tried to lean up on his elbows, only to fall back onto the soft mattress with a tired groan. "Or bits of me in any case."

"Good broken or bad broken?"

"The best kind." Freddie brought his arm up to cover his eyes, and his jaw cracked with a wide yawn. "Would it be the pinnacle of laziness to have a nap at nine in the morning?"

"Yes."

His arm dropped to his side. "Brilliant. I'm having one."

Taine rolled towards the edge of the bed and slowly got to his feet. "You nap. I'm showering all this well-earned sweat off my body."

"Wake me up when you're done." Freddie didn't so much as open his eyes to glance his direction.

Pausing midstep, Taine watched Freddie from by the door to the en-suite. His eyes lingered along the flesh showing outside of the duvet that had been haphazardly dragged across him. He found the young nurse charming—a bit too much so for the sake of his sanity.

A quick cold shower did wonders for his state of mind. Taine wanted a clear head to handle the rest of the day. No matter how casual the sex might've started as, one could never guarantee it would remain so.

The exchange of bodily fluids tended to befuddle even the sternest of characters. He only had to consider two of his closest friends for examples. BC and Caddock had both been firmly in the bachelor category until recently. A bit of pleasure, a smart younger man, and suddenly they'd fallen head over arse in love.

He shook his head violently and sent water flying across the shower. His hands readily found the tap to turn it off. He wouldn't be following in his friends' footsteps—no matter how charming the man or how brilliant the sex.

The Sin Bin aside, Taine intended to fill his post-career days with helping to coach at Cardiff University and working with his charities. The nightclub would be a distraction, but he'd done worse things for his teammates.

Taine grabbed a towel to wipe off his face and then ran it over the nearby mirror. He stared at his reflection. "You've known him since July. It's been a handful of months. Talking like this is what got Caddock and BC into trouble, so stop it."

There, I've told myself, haven't I?
Bollocks.

CHAPTER NINETEEN

FREDDIE

When Gen had forced him into a holiday, Freddie hadn't imagined he would have company. Losing his virginity had also not been a part of the plan. Yet, he couldn't find a single reason to feel disappointed over how things were turning out.

After lounging in bed for a few hours, Freddie wandered into the en-suite to rinse off the sweat and lube from his body. He ignored the deep chuckle from Taine at the slight hitch in his step. The man didn't need—and wouldn't get—an ego boost from him.

Freddie wrapped a fluffy towel around his waist and returned to the bedroom. He had no idea where his pyjamas had gone when Taine tossed them earlier. "Are you hungry? I'm starved. I could eat entire blocks of cheese."

"What's with you and cheese?" Taine set the room phone down on the receiver. "You eat enough of it to lock your system up for months."

"As a medical professional, I feel I should inform you that's not quite how it works." He moved closer to the bed. "Also, cheese is brilliant."

"Sound argument." Taine stretched a long arm out to grab the edge of his towel and yank on it. "I ordered breakfast for us."

"More like brunch." Freddie glanced at the nearby clock to check the time—well past eleven in the morning. "Definitely more brunchish than breakfast. What'd you order? Does it have cheese?"

"I got a delivery from Toastable. They make sandwiches. You'll be overjoyed to know they have a double-cheese-triple-layered sarnie. I got a few others for us to nosh on and, for an extra tip, the lad'll grab two large coffees for us." He grinned when Freddie sent up a prayer of thanks. "Shouldn't you be offering that to me?"

The lad turned out to be a young woman with impressively bright pink hair. She giggled at Taine and winked at Freddie before handing over a large bag along with two cups. They could hear her chattering away into her phone on the way down.

Gossiping.

The same in any language, any race, any sex—people love to share a cute story.

"Catch." Taine tossed a paper-wrapped sandwich to him after foraging around in the bag. "We made an impression on her."

"I'm sure being half-starkers didn't help." Freddie belatedly realised they'd forgotten to throw shirts on before opening the door. He still had the towel wrapped firmly around his waist. "Did you tip well?"

"Always."

Life had taught Freddie you could learn a lot about someone by how they treated serving staff, cashiers, and the like. Taine had, thus far, gone out of his way to be kinder to those others often viewed as less worthy. He considered it an excellent indicator of the depth of goodness in the man.

All right, drink more coffee, Freddie. You're getting too deep this morning. Sex is going to your head.

"Are you sore?"

Freddie blinked a few times, trying to process the question. *Sore?* "Oh. *Oh.* A bit. Nothing major, no pain or anything, it twinges. You are a bit more sizeable than the average bloke."

"Is that a roundabout way of saying my ferret's extra large?" Taine grinned over the rim of his coffee cup. "A ferret who lifts weights?"

"Eat your sarnie." Freddie took a bite of his own sandwich. He enjoyed the chewiness and saltiness of the melted cheeses. He thought it included two types of cheddar and perhaps gouda. The third cheese eluded him. "The cheese market should be open. Are you ready for a tour in the world of dairy?"

Taine peered into his coffee with a seriousness that started to worry Freddie. Those golden eyes finally lifted to meet his brown ones. "Your love of all things cheesy is slightly terrifying. Am I going to have to restrain you?"

"Only in bed." Freddie shot the response back at him without considering the words. He snickered when Taine choked on a sip of coffee. "Problem?"

"Careful with your teasing, Frederick." Taine set the cup down on the nightstand next to a half-eaten sandwich. He strode purposefully across the room to capture Freddie's wrists and pin them behind his back. His teeth caught Freddie's bottom lip to tug on it. "I've always played with a full toy box. Don't taunt me if you're not prepared for the reaction."

"Promise?" Freddie had no idea why he'd decided to yank the tiger by the tail. Taine frankly reminded him more of a sabretooth tiger than an average feline one might find in the jungle. "You're making me hard—I can't deal with that right now."

Taine slid his arm between their bodies to grasp Freddie's hardening shaft, loosely covered by a fluffy white bath towel. "I keep my promises, Frederick. I'll have you all tangled up in a sexual fever so hot that it'll take days for you to think straight."

"'M not straight." Freddie managed to mumble through the haze of arousal. "Also, still hungry."

"Eat your sodding cheese toastie." Taine released him after a bruising kiss. "And when you've finished, we'll go see even more cheese. We'll have the stuff coming out of our ears."

"The good stuff." His mouth started to water just thinking about what he might find in Alkmaar. "You should eat up. I'll tire you out today."

"Will you?" Taine saluted him with the coffee cup he'd picked up again. "We'll see."

CHAPTER TWENTY

TAINE

How much cheese can one man eat in a day?

On the way to Alkmaar, Freddie had explained how the market usually ran until the end of September, but had been extended into the first week of October; they'd only just made the cut. He'd never been able to attend before. The nurse practically vibrated with excitement on the train seat beside him.

After tooling around the various stalls, Freddie dragged him to the Cheese Museum. *Who has a museum dedicated to cheese? And who visits it? Apparently me.* Taine could honestly say it had been the oddest holiday he'd ever had. It included the time Scottie had dragged him to Lancaster County, Pennsylvania, in the US, to visit Gnome Countryside.

He's never picking the holiday spot again—ever.

Three hours into their excursion to Alkmaar, Taine knew everything about making cheese. If it hadn't been for the excited gleam in Freddie's eyes, he might've found the nearest pub for a beer. He probably would if he had to try another yellow square of the squishy dairy nugget.

God—and Freddie—appeared to have mercy on him. They wandered away from the museum and market to hop on a bus across town to eat something other than cheese. Taine had never been more grateful to find a steakhouse in his life.

Steak.

Glorious steak.

"Enjoying your meat?" Freddie asked innocently.

"Of course." Taine nodded. He couldn't help prodding his dinner partner a little. "I'll enjoy yours later."

Freddie coughed on a bite of food. He glared at Taine while choking down water. "Was that necessary?"

"Definitely."

With their early supper out of the way, Taine opted to call for a taxi instead of taking the train to return to Amsterdam. He made sure to spread his legs farther apart than necessary. His thigh pressed against Freddie's and his hand rested on the man's knee.

Freddie folded his arms across his chest while he lifted a single eyebrow, as if to say "Really? Now?"

Taine allowed his fingers to drift up from the knee along the inner seam of the faded jeans the younger man wore. He pressed hard enough to be felt through the thick denim. Freddie inhaled sharply when his hand reached the inner thigh.

"Something the matter?"

"You're an arse." Freddie's eyes darted towards the driver, who appeared focused on the evening traffic. "You can't wait the thirty minutes to get to the hotel?"

"Is your ferret thirsty?" Taine asked with a perfectly serene tone. He'd mastered the art of wiping any sign of amusement from his face early in life. "I'm thirsty for it."

Freddie covered his face with his hands, and his shoulders started to shake with suppressed laughter. "*Twmffat.*"

The amusement didn't last long at all. Taine silenced him by giving up on pretence and trailing his fingers up to the crux of his thighs. They immediately found the bulge in Freddie's jeans.

Bullseye.

His knuckles repeatedly rubbed over it. Freddie kept his hands over his face, though likely for a different reason. His legs felt tense, as if he wanted to shift around on the leather seat of the taxi.

When the driver pulled up in front of the Seven Bridges Hotel, Freddie practically bolted from the vehicle. Taine paid the fare and followed at a far more sedate pace. He reached his room only to find his travelling companion had returned to his own instead.

Deciding a shower would help to rinse off the day—and the cheese—Taine stripped down quickly to his pants and socks, only to be interrupted by a knock on the door. He found Freddie on the other side. The younger man stepped inside, only to stop when he noticed the lack of clothing.

"Did I interrupt?"

"I need a hot shower to wash off the smell of dairy," Taine teased him. "Want to join me?"

The nurse moved towards him as if hypnotised. Freddie reached down to grip the hem of his T-shirt to tug it over his head. He had obviously discarded his jacket in his room.

Shoes were kicked off and across the room, and jeans and socks landed on top of the T-shirt until Freddie stood in nothing but his boxers. Taine had to admire his complete confidence in himself—and lack of insecurity.

Not many of the men or women Taine had been with would've so casually stripped down to nothing. He wondered if Freddie's line of work had made him immune to the almost inborn fear of nudity a staggering number of adults suffered with. Taine certainly wouldn't complain.

Freddie grinned cheekily up at Taine. "Sure we're going to fit? You're a tad bulky."

"Bulky?" Taine ran a hand across his broad chest. "Bulk? This is all muscle."

"Still bulky." Freddie strolled casually towards the en-suite. "Must be a rugby thing."

It wasn't until the shower turned on that Taine started towards the bathroom. He'd been thrown by the teasing from Freddie. The happy bunny hadn't shown off his mischievous side quite so obviously before now.

Leaning against the doorframe, Taine watched the supple, tattooed figure through the glass door of the shower. Steam hadn't obscured him quite yet. The view had his body vibrating with lust almost instantly.

Discarding his pants and socks, Taine eased himself into

the shower. While not a tight squeeze, it did squash them together—rather conveniently and enjoyably. Freddie backed up against the tile wall across from the glass door.

Taine ducked his head under the water to enjoy the warmth. He refocused his attention on the man next to him. Throwing an arm around Freddie to drag him against his body, his lips descended immediately on the attractive neck that was slick with water and vulnerable to him.

He nuzzled up until their lips connected. His legs bent slightly to keep them mouth to mouth. He pursued the caress with a possessively feral edge.

With his knee shoved between Freddie's legs, Taine deepened the kiss. He grinned against the soft mouth when the younger man practically ground himself into his thigh. Their hands explored skin slippery with moisture, and they barely took the time to breathe.

Their cocks both jutted out from their bodies. Freddie's shaft pressed against Taine's thigh. The younger man made small but desperate thrusts while straddling his leg.

Taine pulled both his mouth and leg away from Freddie, earning a hiss of disapproval. He grasped the short brown hair on the man and applied pressure to guide him down to his knees away from the water. His cock nudged against the sinfully swollen lips. "*Suck.*"

When Freddie opened his mouth to respond, Taine pushed forward, his head easily slipping past those wet lips. He kept a firm grip on the short brown hair to control the pace.

Twisting his leg to the side, Taine made sure to rub his foot against the hanging arousal between Freddie's thighs.

He wanted the nurse primed for what would come next. Pun intended.

"That's it, Frederick." Taine nudged forward inch by inch, enjoying the velvet, slick warmth of Freddie's mouth. "Does the weight of it feel good on your tongue?"

Freddie peered up at him, brown eyes darkening with arousal. His hand roamed up Taine's thigh to reach his abdomen. His nails raked across Taine's stomach, causing his muscles to tense.

Taine waited until his balls tightened to yank himself out of those tempting lips. He stroked himself with short, hard tugs until his enjoyment splattered across Freddie's chest. The younger man reached down to stroke himself, only to frown when Taine blocked him with a deft move of his foot. "I've much better plans for you."

After dragging Freddie up to his feet and shoving him under the warm water, Taine turned off the shower and led him out of the bathroom. They didn't bother to dry off. The cool air worked like a strong cup of coffee, leaving both men raring and ready for more.

Water dripped on the floor, trailing a path from the bathroom to the hallway. Taine shoved Freddie down on a sturdy bench in the room. He made quick work of sliding a condom over the younger man's slender but decently long arousal and lubing up the length of him.

Freddie had seemed uneasy with the mechanics of taking Taine's taller and broader form. For his part, he preferred being in control—even with a cock up his arse. It hadn't taken him long to arrive at a solution.

As Freddie sat on the bench with his shaft proudly jutting up into the air, Taine sat down on him. It didn't require any work at all to guide Freddie into him. They both uttered satisfied groans when his bottom rested against those muscled, but lithe legs.

He bounced up and down with all the force his own legs could manage. Freddie's hand drifted around his sides to stroke Taine's cock. His lips wandered along the Maori tattoo of a turtle on his back.

As Freddie had been hard the entire time, it didn't take much for him to explode. Taine lifted up off him almost immediately. He grabbed the younger man and pressed him up against the wall with Freddie's legs wrapped around him.

With his own shaft condom-covered, Taine pushed carefully into Freddie. He pressed one hand on the wall for support and drove up into him. He'd saved his second climax for this reason.

Taine had always been gifted with remarkable stamina. Taking the last of Freddie's cherries had put him on edge, though. He wouldn't require much more stimulus to go off like a rocket again.

His arm wrapped around Freddie to keep the younger man from bashing into the wall with the harder thrusts. Freddie, in turn, looped his arms around Taine's neck. Their lips slipped across one another's in a brushing, lazy sort of dance.

Freddie bounced easily on him with Taine using brute strength to move him up and down. "*God.* It's too much. Too soon. I can't."

Taine bit down on his bottom lip. He'd drawn it out longer

to allow for a bit of recovery time. "You'll be surprised, Frederick, with what your body can manage."

Shifting his angle slightly, Taine zeroed the head of his cock on the sensitised bundle of nerves deep within Freddie. He'd always enjoyed bringing his partners to multiple orgasms. There was always a hint of surprise when a man achieved an orgasm without his cock being overly stimulated.

Freddie's cock had been trapped against Taine's stomach. He could feel it slowly lengthening and hardening. *Almost there.* It had taken immense self-will not to surrender to the pleasure with the younger man's constant heavy panting and moans echoing in his ears.

He had so much to show Freddie. *So many tricks in the toy box.* It had been ages since a sexual partner had fired him up. He couldn't wait to get home and see how adventurous Freddie could be.

From the loud noises that Taine used his hand to muffle, Freddie would be more than open to experimenting. He slowed his thrusts down. It threw the younger man slightly, but not much.

"You ready?" Taine asked before lifting Freddie up and teasing him with the head of his shaft. "Are you, Frederick?"

"*Fel ci a dau goc,*" Freddie managed to murmur.

"Take that as a yes."

And he did.

CHAPTER TWENTY-ONE

For the second time in as many days, Freddie found himself collapsing on a bed in a post-sex haze of exhaustion. He barely managed to summon enough energy to take the warm, wet flannel from Taine to wipe his bits off. They'd already discarded the used condoms in the trash.

His mouth and throat felt sore. He could only hope that while he'd been voicing his pleasure the other hotel guests hadn't been disturbed. Gen would find it incredibly hilarious if he got kicked out of the hotel.

And Gen would find out. The doctor had a frighteningly gifted way of extracting information from him. He'd never managed to successfully keep a secret from the woman.

He could picture the smug grin on her face when he

returned from Amsterdam. She would be insufferable for weeks. "I set you up with the rugby hottie." He could all but hear her crowing in his head.

Maybe I can move to the Netherlands? They have cancer patients here, right? We're still part of the European Union. No one will find it strange.

Everyone will find it strange.

"Think there's a delivery place open now?" Taine dropped onto the mattress like a boulder, which almost launched Freddie into the air. "I've worked up quite an appetite."

Freddie rolled over on his side with a slight wince. His body had relaxed completely, only to tighten up slightly. He'd have to do some stretches before sleeping. "You ate enough to feed a small family at supper. How can you be hungry?"

Taine rubbed his stomach briefly before fumbling blindly on the nightstand for his mobile. "Physical exertion burns calories. Burning calories requires resupplying food."

"In your professional opinion, Manager Afoa?" Freddie could see how the man would make a good coach for a rugby team. He had the sternness to keep them in line, but a good enough sense of humour not to be too hard on them. "So, what's this about the Sin Bin? You never did explain fully."

While Taine explained about the nightclub details, the two perused delivery options on his mobile. They settled on a pizza place that delivered until two in the morning. It had just gone midnight, so they had plenty of time to place the order.

One cheese.

One with meat.

Four beers.

Sitting cross-legged on the edge of the bed, Freddie convinced Taine to play a round of never-have-I-ever after the food had arrived. With a grand total of four beers, the game didn't last long. He'd yet to discover something Taine *hadn't* done.

It made him curious. What all could Taine show him about sex? Given the results of the drinking game—a disturbingly large number of things.

Curiosity killed the bunny.

Maybe sex brings the bunny back?

He giggled to himself. Taine lifted his eyebrows at him, but he only shook his head. It would be far too difficult and weird to explain the inner workings of his mind.

Sated with cheese pizza, beer, and knowledge of amazing sex to come, Freddie collapsed back on the bed. He waved a hand without opening his eyes when Taine asked if he intended to return to his room. He dozed off to the sound of a deep chuckle on the other side of the bed.

The next few days of his impromptu vacation passed by in a similar vein, adventures around the city during the day and wildly exhausting buggering by night. Freddie worried it wouldn't take much to grow far too accustomed to having Taine in his life. He wondered if the rugby player would be interested in going out for dinner in Cardiff—and by dinner, he meant dating and more sex.

Don't get ahead of yourself.

After all, many people screwed around on holiday only to pretend the person didn't exist afterwards. Freddie had seen it done. Gen had told him about a woman who'd dropped her like a sack of potatoes after a whirlwind romance in Rome after a medical convention.

Poor Genevieve. The doctor had the worst luck with dates. Freddie had been only slightly more successful, which wasn't saying much. He tried not to assume maybe this trip to Amsterdam was a sign of a change in his romantic life.

On the train back home, Freddie had found himself instinctively beginning to withdraw. He'd enjoyed the week away. It would be hard to return to his often lonely and always high-pressure life in Cardiff.

His books stayed in his bag. His eyes focused on the scenery speeding by. He refused to glance at the man dozing beside him.

Stop it. You're winding yourself up over nothing. You've enjoyed yourself. Don't act like a stupid child now that you're going home.

By the time they'd swapped trains in Lille, Freddie had managed to resurrect his spirits. They'd found a great café near the station to have coffee and a brilliant cheesy pastry. He'd wanted to take a box of them home with him.

Probably wouldn't travel well.

They grabbed fresh coffee and sandwiches to share on the train. Freddie pulled out a novel he'd picked up in Amsterdam. He might've felt better, but not well enough to be social.

Despite his best efforts, Freddie couldn't help thinking of what he'd left in the Netherlands. *I'm not a virgin. I buggered him. Well, he buggered himself on me. Does it count? It counts. I hope it does. It should. Oh God. Why is he staring at me?*

"You're cute when you ramble to yourself." Taine leaned

across the armrest to murmur against his ear. "It *definitely* counts."

"Oh, kill me now." Freddie grabbed his book to shove it closer to his face to hide his reddening cheeks. He didn't usually blush. "I'll close my eyes, and none of this will have happened."

CHAPTER TWENTY-TWO

TAINE

As they settled into the last leg of the journey to Cardiff after swapping trains in London, Taine could sense the mixed emotions rolling off the man beside him in waves. Freddie had his nose shoved so far into his novel that only part of his forehead was visible. He was definitely hiding from him, the situation, or both.

While happy to let it go for the first bit of their two-hour trip from London to Cardiff, Taine decided the silence had gone on long enough. It didn't take a mystic ability to guess at least part of the source of the issue. He believed he could allay a majority of Freddie's fears.

He dropped his hand on Freddie's knee. "Good book?"

"So far."

"Do you have plans for Sunday night?" Taine asked casually.

"Tomorrow night?" Freddie's brown eyes flickered to his, not quite managing to mask a flash of vulnerability. "No plans. I'm not due in to work until Monday. Bitsy'll want attention. My flat'll need a clean. I should probably call my dads so they know I wasn't chopped into pieces and thrown in a canal."

"How about I come over to cook for you? I make a mean steak and chips." Taine wouldn't admit to it being the one thing he'd mastered in the kitchen. "Might bring a few extras with me, as well."

"Extras?" Freddie's eyes went wide. He shifted in his seat, which made Taine smirk. "*Twmffat.*"

"Thank you." Taine knew enough Welsh now to know he'd been called an idiot. He didn't mind. He got a thrill out of eliciting such an immediate reaction out of Freddie. *Careful, Taine, your Dom side is showing.* "So, supper? Tomorrow? Say around seven?"

Freddie nodded sharply and immediately buried his face in his book once again. Taine relaxed into the quiet to consider how to ease the man into a conversation about some of his sexual preferences. He belatedly released his firm grip on the knee he'd taken possession of earlier.

A little over two hours found them arriving at the Cardiff train station. Freddie had left his car at home, so Taine offered him a lift. He somehow ended up following him up to his flat. In the end, he was glad his instincts had urged him to do it.

Ripped blue tape lay around on the floor by the door of his flat. The smell of fresh paint filled the air. Something had quite obviously happened.

It didn't take a genius to figure out the homophobic twats had returned. The new paint on the door indicated what they'd done. Taine watched Freddie's normally cheerful expression crumple in an instant.

The younger man moved rather mechanically forward to shove his key into the lock and open the door. Taine kicked the police tape to the side, and they stepped into the flat.

"I'm so tired of people's hatred. It drains all the happiness from the world." Freddie tossed his keys blindly to the side, missing the table by the door and hitting the floor instead. He collapsed on the couch with one hand absently stroking his cat, who hopped up into his lap. "I thought Cardiff would be a wonderful start to living life on my own. It's turning into the worst sort of nightmare."

Letting Freddie vent his anguish, Taine picked up a note from the welcome mat. It had clearly been shoved underneath the door. The landlord had apparently caught the teens in the act and called the police, who would be by on Sunday for a chat.

Taine sat next to Freddie and wrapped an arm around his tense shoulders. "Police caught them."

"They'll be out to harass me soon enough," he huffed hopelessly. "Always are."

One couldn't necessarily argue with him. The way the laws read, the most someone would get for a hate crime would likely be a fine and up to six months imprisonment.

Thus far, he knew the juvenile offenders had been fined. A court might lock them up this time, but it would place Freddie in the same exact spot afterwards.

Bastards.

The sad truth of the matter was, if the two idiots had attacked Freddie over being Jewish, they'd likely have received a harsher punishment. *Unfair.* The world around them didn't necessarily offer the same protections when it came to matters of sexual preference.

"Move." Taine kept his voice firm but gentle. "There are much better areas of the city to live."

Freddie shrugged.

"You could ask Graham's brother to give you a hand. He's a land agent in Cornwall. He'll know someone local you could talk to." Taine would be giving the man a call himself no matter what Freddie decided to do. "What can it hurt?"

Freddie gave another half-hearted lift of his shoulders. "Why must people be so completely vicious? I've done nothing to them. I barely know them."

"How about I fix you that steak tonight?" Taine tugged him closer, his arm squeezing tightly to offer comfort. "Or cheese? Is there some secret cheese club I can take you to where you can swim in the stuff?"

"Swim in cheese?" Freddie's smile might've been dimmed, but at least it was there. "What a waste of the good stuff. What kind would work as a pool?"

"No idea." Taine ran his fingers along the edge of his jaw, scratching underneath his beard for a moment. "What's in your fridge?"

"Not much." Freddie pushed up to his feet, cradling his cat in his arms. He trudged into the kitchen to open the fridge and stare gloomily into it. "I've got some dodgy leftovers, cheese, more cheese, all the cheese."

"Dodgy leftovers?" Taine joined him in the kitchen. He leaned over his shoulders to look in, making sure to press his upper body against Freddie's back. "Is that soup? Who keeps soup leftovers?"

"What's wrong with soup?" Freddie tilted his head around to the side and inhaled slightly when their lips practically grazed together. "It's good stuff."

"We're not having dodgy soup." Taine looped his arms around Freddie's waist and shifted him away from the fridge, allowing the door to swing shut. "How about a takeaway? What're you in the mood to have?"

"Something to cheer me up." Freddie wiggled out of his embrace, Bitsy meowing in protest at being shuffled in her comfortably purring state. "How about Happy House Takeaway? They've a brilliant beef curry."

They noshed on curry and watched *Doctor Who* reruns until the day of travelling caught up with them. Taine didn't even realise he'd fallen asleep until a sandpaper tongue licked his cheek. He batted away Bisty and glanced down at the man asleep beside him with his head in Taine's lap.

It feels far earlier than seven in the morning.

Rousing Freddie from his sleep, Taine promised to come by later for supper. He had to check on his own apartment— and Speedy. Scottie had promised to check in on his hamster, but one could never be certain how the man would take to responsibility of any type.

Not well, usually.

And BC wants him to run a nightclub with all of our names attached to it?

Shite.

Both his house and hamster were thankfully unharmed by their week in Scottie's dubious care. Taine would have to send the man a bottle of whisky by way of gratitude. He filled his massive Jacuzzi tub and sank into it. The strains of his blues playlist played in the background.

He considered the week away to have been a success. His mind and body had definitely needed space to relax. He could approach starting as a part-time coach for the Cardiff University rugby team with more energy and enthusiasm.

Sinking further into the warm water, Taine rested his head on the edge of the bath. His time post retirement had sped up and slowed down in equal measures. It felt more like November or December, not mid-October.

A buzzing from the floor had him reaching down to fish his mobile out of his trousers pocket. BC wanted to know how his seduction had gone. *Knobdobber.* A message from Scottie had a similar question in with a far more vulgar phrasing. *Why are these people my friends?*

Remi: Tens? Sarah wants you to bring your new boyfriend for dinner. Didn't know you'd moved to relationship from one holiday? You haven't, have you? You're not that desperate.

Taine: I'm not desperate at all. Thanks for that. Did you want something other than to join the others in taking the piss?

Remi: Dinner? Next week? Bring the kid.

Taine: He's a grown man.

Remi: You'd know, wouldn't you?

Taine: If I wanted this shite, I would've answered Scottie's text. I'll see if Freddie's interested.

Of all his friends, Remi would be the one least likely to offend Freddie. The Frenchie and his wife were good people. He would enjoy supper with them—whether the young nurse joined them or not.

He found himself hoping Freddie would want to join him. *Not my boyfriend, barely my lover, but nothing wrong with hoping that it might evolve into something.* He splashed water into his face. Shaking his head to clear his eyes, it became clear his mind and his cock were of one mind when it came to the lithe form of the twenty-six-year-old.

Sliding one hand along his chest into the water to wrap around his semihard shaft, Taine allowed his thoughts to drift to some of the toys in his closet and how he might use them on Freddie. He had a special set of restraints he'd always wanted to try out. His cock went from semi to fully aroused just imagining it.

The water splashed around him. It lapped against the now sensitive head like a constant tease. His fingers nimbly stroked to a steady rhythm.

With his eyes closed, Taine pictured Freddie stretched out on his bed. His pale olive skin would contrast beautifully with the navy silk sheets. His wrists would be cuffed to the iron headboard and his legs forced apart with the metal spreader.

What a stunning visual.

He could readily imagine the pink lines along his arse

from where Taine had spanked him. His shaft twitched almost painfully with the thought of enjoying Freddie's pert bottom. If the younger man enjoyed stories so much, they would pen a bestseller together in his bedroom.

As Taine lost himself in fantasies of what might happen, his hand sped up rapidly. His fingers tightened around his shaft. He spent his release in the bath water—a fire burning in his belly to implement even a portion of his imaginings.

Once the tub had drained, Taine hopped out and grabbed a towel to dry off. He strolled into his bedroom and straight over to the antique chest at the foot of his bed. It contained all the toys best kept away from prying eyes.

All right, which toys say, "I came to play," but won't terrify the curiosity out of him?

CHAPTER TWENTY-THREE

FREDDIE

Once Taine had left for his flat, Freddie fed Bitsy, showered, and did a quick clean of his bedroom. He had a feeling the rugby player would be spending at least some time in there with him. With the dodgy food tossed from his fridge, he popped around to the local shop to replenish his supplies.

Over a simple lunch of stew that had been brought over by one of his neighbours, Freddie checked on his work emails. Nothing important had arrived while he'd swanned off to Amsterdam. Genevieve had a new client for him to see on Tuesday—a nineteen-year-old with a brain tumour.

God help him.

Dumping the bowl into his sink to wash later, Freddie grabbed his laptop and sat on the floor with Bitsy pouncing on his socked feet randomly. The next week would be a bit of a long one. He had too many things to catch up on, one of the many reasons why he'd never taken a week of vacation.

Freddie had opened his online calendar app to begin organising his week when his mobile gave a cheerful ring. "Dad."

"Hello, love." His dad tended to get straight to the point, unlike his husband. "Are you joining us for Yom Kippur?"

Ahh.

"You know I don't celebrate." Freddie cringed at the sigh he could hear on the other end. His fathers had always been rather open about their differing religious beliefs. Their Jewish relatives and Protestant ones had rarely agreed on anything. He had been left to decide how to worship on his own as a result. "You'll only get upset with me."

"You don't have to worship to enjoy the dinner we have together, son." His dad managed to guilt him without actually chastising him. *It's a gift, must be.* "Your auntie said you went on a holiday to Amsterdam with a friend?"

"Yes." Freddie squeezed his eyes shut and prayed his aunt hadn't known any of the details. "How'd she know?"

"Dr Williams."

Oh. No.

There was a scuffle on the other end of the line. "Who was your friend?" his tad asked. The scuffle had obviously been a struggle for the phone. "Someone new in your life? Your aunt couldn't get any information—not even a name."

No, no, no, no.

Freddie aimed for calm and confident. "No one you know."

"So, someone new from Cardiff? Tell us about your friend, love." His dad had regained control of his phone. "What's their name?"

"Taine Afoa."

For a moment, no one said anything. The silence was followed immediately by a shout of excitement and the phone being snatched again. His tad exclaimed into the phone about him meeting a rugby player.

Freddie thought for several minutes he would get away without any of the more pertinent and dangerous questions being asked. "I met him through Graham's BC. You remember, Boyce Brooks?"

"Of course I—"

His dad cut off his husband with another fight for the phone. "Freddie, why precisely did Tens Afoa go to Amsterdam with you? How long have you known the man? You couldn't have been friends for long. He retired this year."

Coc y gath.

"Freddie?"

He knew he'd have to give an answer of some sort. "I met him in July at the hospital."

Not a lie. I didn't know him then, but I met him.

"So, three months and you're going on holiday together?" His father's voice had a definite note of disapproval. "How old is he? He's got to be close to our age."

"*Dad.*"

"When can we meet him?"

Never.

"We're only friends." Freddie didn't honestly know what

to call the budding connection with Taine. He certainly had no interest in dissecting it with his overprotective fathers. "Friends."

"Methinks our son doth protest too much."

"Twice. I said it twice." Freddie muted his phone and yelled "Why?" at the ceiling before returning to the conversation. "Do you remember what happened the last time I brought a friend to the farm? Do you? Hmm?"

"The lad has a point." His dad couldn't argue, though he'd probably try. "We enjoy meeting all of your friends, love. Why is this one different?"

"*Dad.*"

Another fight for the phone.

"Are you dating him?"

Freddie winced at the question from his tad, who had always been a little more intuitive of the two men. "I've only known him since July."

"The absence of a simple no leads me to believe you are— or are hoping to date him. How old is Taine Afoa? I recall reading an article about him in the paper the other day. They said he'd been one of the oldest players left in the game before retiring." He didn't leave any room for his son to wiggle out of the direction of the conversation. "We're having a big lunch on Sunday a fortnight from today. You'll bring Mr Afoa for us to meet."

Oh, shit.

"Don't you curse me mentally, young man." His tad laughed. "You have a good morning, love."

Freddie stared in horror at his now silent phone. "Well, there's the end of that relationship, and it's not even started."

His fathers had never been brilliant about his dates, one of many reasons Freddie's move to Cardiff couldn't have come at a better time. His hope to avoid their antics had clearly been for naught.

They usually interfered in the most humiliating ways imaginable. Freddie still cringed over the time they'd driven out to his university to ensure his eating habits were healthy. His classmates had mocked him mercilessly for an entire year over it.

The solution to the problem usually involved calling his aunt, who would drag her brother and brother-in-law back into some semblance of sanity. Freddie didn't know how she would respond to the idea of him dating a man in his forties. It still seemed far too soon to be considering meeting the family or even simply calling it more than a casual date.

He had two weeks to figure out how to avoid the catastrophe. Time to hang around the emergency ward at the hospital; someone was bound to have the flu. He could come down with a suddenly terminal case of the plague.

What am I going to do?

Freddie frowned at Bitsy, who stretched in the sun before leaping up onto the couch to curl up. "This is going to be a nightmare, isn't it?"

Meow.

"Yes, yes it is."

CHAPTER TWENTY-FOUR

TAINE

Sunday evening came far too quickly. Taine barely managed to see to catching up with everything from being gone for a week. He found time to get a trim of his hair and beard—no need to look like a barbarian, even if he planned to act like one.

Lunch with Scottie should've been skipped. The man injected every other sentence with an insinuation of one sort or another. It reminded Taine of how his *friend* had once described himself to a sports journo: "Scott's a bit of a tosser, but Scottie is a complete and utter wanker."

Today had been Scottie at his worst. Taine cared deeply for his old teammate, but enough was enough. He'd left him at the restaurant with the tab. Shaking off the uneasy energy, he focused on preparing for what would hopefully be a far more enjoyable evening.

With a bag of raw ingredients in his right hand and another in his left with less edible treats, Taine made his way up to Freddie's flat. The nurse wouldn't know what hit him.

He hadn't expected to arrive to find the generally happy bunny frazzled—and jumpy, the perfect word to describe his mood.

Not good.

Any query into why garnered him a blank but slightly embarrassed expression. *Time to move the conversation on to better topics.* The mood would have to be lifted for anything even remotely enjoyable to happen. Spending the night suffering from stress-induced indigestion wasn't on his to-do list.

Taking command of Freddie's iPod, Taine thumbed through the playlists to find one with a somewhat decent collection of blues and jazz. He hit Play, set the gadget down, and caught the man's arm to drag him over. His attempt at smoothly dancing the bad energy away ended pathetically with his partner hopping around on one foot.

"Do you even know how to dance?" Freddie rubbed the tips of his toes gingerly.

"Mostly. How hard can it be?" Taine hadn't thought it a hard skill to fake. "I can haka."

"Not exactly a slow dance, is it? Are you planning on going to war tonight?" Freddie wiggled his toes before kicking off his other shoe as well. He grabbed one of Taine's hands to rest on his shoulder and put the other arm loosely around his waist. "This song? Close your eyes and feel the gentle, airy depths of the melody. It's a blast of warm air after a muggy rain. You move with it, not against it. Think about running on a pitch, smoothly spinning around your opponents, aiming for a match-winning try. Sway with the music—hit the gentle staccato of the bass. There. See? You can do it."

Taine wound his arm more closely around Freddie's back. He let the magic of the moment carry them away until the song ended. Fingers gripping his shirt stopped him from pulling away.

Apparently, we'll be going for at least one more tune.

They made it through two and a half songs before Bitsy wove between their legs and tripped them up. Taine caught Freddie just in time to stop him tumbling headfirst into the wall. He chuckled at the muttered, "Menace of a cat. No tuna for you. Ruining the moment."

Deciding they'd faffed off enough, Taine grabbed the bag of food. The steak would be cooked and eaten. He would be able to handle meat of a different variety much later.

"Right. Are you ready to play sous chef for me?" Taine turned on one of the burners on the hob. "Do you have a baking pan?"

"My hands are yours—as are my pans." Freddie darted into the kitchenette before Taine. He rushed around, pulling out accoutrements that he obviously believed would be required to prepare their supper. "I've beer and a bottle of wine. Gen bought it for me as a housewarming present."

Taine glanced over at the bottle. He recognised the vintage from one Caddock and Francis had shared with him once, and gave a low whistle. "Expensive wine. You not a fan? I'd have drunk it by now."

Freddie shrugged indifferently. "Never cared much either way."

"We'll have it with supper." Taine returned his attention to unpacking the ingredients. He'd be making an ale-glazed steak with garlic parmesan seasoned chips. He handled the knife deftly on the potatoes. "Can you preheat the oven to gas mark six? These need to bake for a good bit to turn into strips of golden joy."

The strains of Billie Holiday filtered through the flat while they found an easy companionship in the kitchen. Taine purposefully bumped into or brushed against Freddie repeatedly—always intentionally. He intended for him to have as heightened a sense of awareness as possible.

Little touches here and there; his hand grazed across Freddie's arse more than once. By the time both the steak and chips had cooked, the younger man appeared far more flushed than the cramped nature of the kitchen would make him. An obvious bulge in his trousers indicated the source of his overheating.

The round dining table played right into his plans. Taine ensured his leg pressed against Freddie's. After cutting up his own steak for easy eating, he dropped his hand high up on the younger man's upper thigh; his fingertips grazed over the fabric-covered arousal.

"Are you quite happy with yourself?" Freddie glared at him but did nothing to dislodge the hand now directly over his shaft. "I'll break a tooth on my fork if you keep making me jump."

Taine squeezed him firmly in response. "How's your steak?"

"Perfect." Freddie tried to lift Taine's hand out of the way, but he managed to twist it around so now the man caressed his own cock. "Is the plan to actually cause me to lose my mind over the course of supper?"

Taine grinned wolfishly when the heated arousal under their joined fingers twitched. "Eat up, Frederick. You're going to need your strength."

Freddie snagged one of the chips and shoved it into his mouth with exaggeratedly precise movements. He chewed with almost comical slowness. "Is this torture by supper?"

"No, it's foreplay."

CHAPTER TWENTY-FIVE

Despite the delicious aromas of the meal, Freddie barely tasted any of the food passing his lips. He should've felt in charge—in control—with them being in his flat. Taine had arrived with an aura of pure dominance; Freddie savoured the intoxicating nature of it far more than any drug or alcohol.

There had been hints of a dangerous depth in the undercurrents of their sexual encounters throughout the holiday in Amsterdam, subtle gestures that teased him. Yet, nothing over the week had strayed too far out of what could be termed vanilla.

How am I supposed to focus with a hand massaging my John Thomas?

Bitsy, the traitor, had fallen in love with Taine. She

currently lay stretched out behind his chair on a rug. Crazy cat loved the treats his guest brought for her.

Bribing bastard.

Finicky feline.

"Are you finished?" Taine used his fork to nudged Freddie's plate. "How was your steak?"

"Your hand is on my cock," Freddie bit out when those tricky fingers shifted their grip. "It's a tad distracting. You'll have me biting through my tongue."

Taine continued his manipulation through the grey trousers Freddie wore. "Supper will keep. You seem thirsty for a different kind of sustenance. Do you want to play, Frederick?"

"Play?" Freddie cleared his throat and reached for his glass to gulp down water. He'd decided not to have wine or beer, having guessed a clear head might be useful. "I'm guessing you're not about to teach me the rules of rugby."

"Red means stop. Yellow tells me you want to slow things down. Green's my favourite. It's the signal I need before I show you all the ways to play in bed." Taine shoved his plate away and released his hold on Freddie's arousal. He went into great detail about what his intentions were for the evening, including what toys he'd brought and what being dominated for the first time would be like, obviously not wanting anything to be an unpleasant surprise. "Red, yellow, or green? What'll it be, Frederick?"

Freddie set his fork down and pushed his plate aside. He found the intensity in those blazing gold eyes difficult to meet. *What am I going to do?* "Green."

I'm apparently jumping in the kink pond with both feet.

I'm going to drown.

"You certain?" Taine's tone of voice suggested he wouldn't move forward without knowing Freddie wanted whatever was about to happen. "I can think of a million other things we can do."

"No, green, I'm definitely in the greenish hue." Freddie's anxiety had faded rapidly into excitement. "Won't it give us indigestion?"

"Did you eat enough to worry?" Taine's eyes flicked towards the barely touched meal. "I didn't. We'll be fine. Still green?"

Fine?

How encouraging.

Freddie nodded. "Green."

When Taine mentioned wanting to dip his toes in the water, Freddie didn't quite know what to anticipate. Getting cosily handcuffed to his own bed hadn't even topped his list of possibilities. He suddenly found himself grateful for the thorough cleaning in his earlier shower.

Not cuffed, tied. Taine proved to be remarkably gifted with rope. Each step of the way, the man had questioned him with "red, green, yellow?" Freddie had a knotted loop around each wrist and ankle, spreading his body across his bed. His head rested on a pillow, elevated slightly to provide a better view.

Or, it had.

Taine approached with a handful of fabric. He placed a yellow scarf in Freddie's left hand and a red one in his right. The reasoning became clear once a blindfold covered his eyes and noise-cancelling headphones blocked the sound from his ears.

The first touch made him jump—not far given the ropes. Freddie never imagined how much the loss of sight and sound would heighten his sense of touch. A flick to one of his nipples hit like an electric shock all the way down his spine, straight to his cock.

His shaft hardened to full staff and almost immediately something cold slid down the length of it. Whatever the circle was snapped shut at the base. *Cock ring.* He could only imagine how delightfully torturous the evening could be.

The flicking stopped only for it to turn to pinching and tugging. *Have I always had a nipple fetish?* Coc y gath. He bit his lip to stop a moan when a hand wrapped firmly around his arousal to give it a few rough strokes.

Touch left his nipples, and his bottom lip was pulled from between his teeth. *Message received.* Taine clearly wanted to not only see but hear the results of his play. Freddie hoped it wouldn't end up bringing the neighbours down on them.

With no concept of time passing, Freddie writhed with every teasing touch. The hands disappeared. He froze on the bed, wondering what would come next.

Not me.

Damn ring.

Lubed fingers circled down below. Freddie couldn't help holding his breath when they delved into him. One gentle thrusting digit was followed almost immediately by two, stretching and dipping further into him.

The ropes kept him from lifting up to meet the daring invaders. He wanted to do it. His body hummed with a hunger for more of everything.

The restraints on his ankles were removed. Freddie felt the bed shift before an arm wrapped around his legs to tilt him up, practically folding him in half. His arse went up in the air, vulnerable to Taine's large hand, which landed heavily on one cheek.

Rough, calloused fingers trailed casually along his crease. They disappeared. In the darkened silence, all he could do was wait for the inevitable.

Taine rained glancing swats on his arse, not too hard, but certainly not soft by any measure. Freddie never imagined the growing heat down below could make him even more painfully aroused. He mentally cursed the ring preventing it.

As if Taine read his mind, the spanking stopped right at the moment it would've gone from pleasurable to simply painful. The headset was yanked from his head and the blindfold along with the restraints on his wrists were more gently removed. He blinked in the sudden brightness of his bedroom.

"Are we happily in green?" Taine lowered Freddie's legs to the bed. He flipped him over on his stomach, catching him by the hips to ease him up on his knees. "Green?"

Freddie managed to nod. He might have to kill the man if he had the gall to stop now. His body had never been so hard and ready to explode.

In a bit of a daze, Freddie barely noticed Taine climbing on the bed behind him. He heard the ripping of a condom wrapper. With the headphones off his ears, every sound struck him as if the volume had been turned all the way up to the maximum.

Freddie pressed his lips together to halt the steady stream of "green, green, green, green" that he'd been uttering without realising it. "Take this off. *Please.*"

"This?" Taine slid a hand underneath him to tug on his shaft, running a finger all around the ring keeping Freddie prisoner. "Want it gone?"

Freddie glared over his shoulder at the man, earning a yank to his hair. "*Off.*"

"My hand or the ring?"

"Guess."

Three things happened one right after the other. Taine began to press his lubed and condom-covered cock forward into Freddie. He swatted his arse once. And he reached underneath to tug off the ring.

In his wildest imagination, Freddie never thought one could black out from the power of an orgasm. He must've. The next moment of awareness had him lying on his back with Taine beside him.

All the toys and other items were gone from the bed. Taine had obviously cleaned up the lube and evidence of their joint pleasure. Freddie blinked up at the bedroom ceiling, trying to remember how to breathe and speak.

"You've hidden depths." Freddie shoved the blanket off his body. "Also, I'm fairly confident I came so hard I pulled a muscle in my cock."

"Want me to massage it better?"

"No." Freddie rolled out of the way of the hand wandering towards him. "I'm going to see if Bitsy left any of the steaks for us."

"Frederick?"

He twisted around at the door to peer over his shoulder at Taine, who was slowly getting off the bed. "Yes?"

"We're good, right?"

"*Green.*"

CHAPTER TWENTY-SIX

TAINE

After tugging on his boxers, Taine wandered through the flat to the kitchen. He didn't want to leave Freddie on his own for long. Being even casually dominated for the first time could throw anyone for a loop.

Freddie stood by the counter with a beer in one hand and a strip of steak in his other. He grinned before grabbing a bite of the meat. "Hungry?"

"I see you've found your appetite again." Taine handed over a pair of briefs he'd snagged from the dresser. "Wouldn't want you to catch a cold."

"Oh yes, a pair of pants usually keeps me warm at night." Freddie took a swig of beer. "Want a bottle?"

Taine strode across the room to loop his arm around

Freddie's shoulders. "You doing okay? Not shaky or anything?"

"Am I supposed to be?" He shrugged before taking another bite. "I'm hungry."

"Would you do it again?" Taine found himself hoping for a yes. He'd played with several partners casually and explored some of the clubs in London. It had never been with anyone who he might consider more than a once-off. "Maybe go a little further? Do a bit more?"

"Green." Freddie grinned cheekily at him. "Maybe not immediately. I'm still convinced I sprained something."

Ahh, good. Wouldn't it have been utter shite if he said no?

The two men stood in the kitchen, eating steak and cold chips with their fingers. They shared the beer as well.

It was a bit more domestic than Taine usually went with his sex partners. Freddie, even as young and bunny-like as he was, brought a calmness with him. It became almost stupidly easy to relax in his presence.

A quick peek at his watch told him that they'd gone much later than intended. He'd arrived around seven, and now it was almost two in the morning. Time apparently flew when one had someone tied up in bed.

"Want trifle?"

"Trifle?" Taine asked after swallowing the last bite of steak. "What type?"

"The 'whatever is in my fridge' kind." Freddie yanked open the door to his refrigerator and peered inside. He jolted forward into it when Taine swatted his arse. "Oi!"

"Problem?"

Freddie leaned back to reveal a chin covered in custard. "You knocked me right into one of the trifle layers."

Taine grabbed him by the head, fingers tightening around his hair to ease him up. He bent slightly to allow himself the tasty pleasure of licking all the delightfully sweet custard from Freddie's face. "Delicious."

"*Twmffat.*"

"How about we dump all the ingredients on your body and I eat it off you?" Taine made a mental note to buy custard, whipped cream, and chocolate at the shop. He'd definitely be experimenting with all the yummy things it might be fun to use to cover Freddie's body. "No?"

"Oh God." Freddie winced visibly. "Don't tease me. It hurts to get hard."

"Good or bad hurt?" Taine lifted a knee up to rub it against the younger man's pert arse. He smirked at the sudden hiss. "I'm guessing the former."

"Bit of both." Freddie moved away from the fridge with several bowls balanced in his arms. "Could you help? I'd rather not clean glass off the floor."

Taine grabbed the custard, leaving Freddie with a bowl of strawberries, raspberries, and a pot of jam. "I can imagine a better use for all of these things."

"I'm sure you can, but you'll restrict yourself to putting them in a dish and eating them." He set two smaller bowls on the counter and grabbed two spoons. "I've shortbread and a vanilla sponge. Any preferences?"

"Both."

"You do enjoy indulging, don't you?" Freddie flicked a

dollop of cream at him. "Naughty, naughty."

Taine rolled his eyes and snagged one of the bowls off the counter. He'd barely had time to lift one spoonful up to his mouth when the unmistakable sound of a key in a lock echoed in the flat. "Expecting someone?"

Freddie gripped the edge of the counter and looked as if he might pass out. "The only people with keys to my flat aside from the landlord would be my dads. I highly doubt it's Neil. He'd call first."

"And your dads wouldn't?"

"Not when they already know I spent a week in Amsterdam with a much older man. Though, I can't for the life of me understand why they'd leave in the middle of the night." Freddie glanced around the room. He appeared to be in a panic. "We're not wearing any clothes."

"Pants."

"Do you think my dads will honestly believe a pair of boxers and a pair of briefs count as being dressed?" Freddie glared at Taine, who continued to casually eat his trifle. "Aren't you worried?"

"I'm a grown man. I stopped worrying about parents a long time ago." He didn't see the point in getting upset. They were both consenting adults. Yes, he'd struggled with the age difference himself, but surely loving parents would want to see their son happy. "Want me to go get our trousers?"

"And walk through the living room without me?" Freddie took a desperate swig of beer. "This will be embarrassing."

"Freddie? *Cariad*? Are you here? We got worried and decided our visit couldn't wait. Where are you?" Footsteps grew closer and closer. A man with the same dark hair and eyes as Freddie came to stand in the entry, staring wide-eyed at the two men in the kitchen. "Adam? They're in here."

"They? What do you mean 'they,' Fred?"

"They."

"Dad. Tad. I'd like you to meet Taine Afoa." Freddie sounded far more sure of himself than he had seconds ago. He gestured towards the two men. "Taine, these are my fathers. Adam and Fred Whittle."

"Pleasure." Taine could see the embers of anger beginning to burn in Fred's eyes. Fred had definitely not been the one to gift his namesake with a calm and cheerful temperament. "We were about to have pudding. Would you care to join us?"

"I'd care for you to get your arse in some trousers before you explain what the hell you're doing in my son's flat. I'd wager you're not five years younger than we are." Fred didn't make it further into the kitchen. His husband caught him by the arm to hold him back, whispering something into his ear. "We'd love to have tea while you finish your supper."

"I'll go get trousers." Freddie squeezed through the small gap between his fathers.

Fred stayed in the kitchen while Adam followed his son. Those muddy brown eyes focused intensely on Taine. "What are you doing here?"

"Enjoying trifle." He refused to be intimated or guilt-tripped. They'd done nothing wrong. "Your son is an impressive man."

"He's a young man."

"Is twenty-six young?" Taine shot back.

"Younger than you by I'd wager at least ten years or more." Fred folded his arms across his chest. He clearly wouldn't back down anytime soon when it came to his son. "I'll ask you again. What do you think you're doing here?"

"Engaging in a completely consensual relationship with an adult." Taine set the bowl aside, not wanting anything in his hands. "Why don't you say what you're thinking?"

"You perverted bastard." Adam returned to the kitchen and flung a handful of rope at Taine. "Get the hell away from my son."

Taine looped the rope around his arm. He'd taken the time to oil it to make sure it was not only pliable but unlikely to chafe. "You are aware your son is a grown man. Shouldn't he be the one to make that decision?"

"You're no better than a paedophile," Fred spat at him.

"*Stop it.*" Freddie's horrified voice came from the living room. He hopped into the kitchen, still trying to get one leg of his jeans up. "Could you give us a moment, Taine?"

Shell-shocked from the accusation thrown at him, Taine could only nod and vacate the room as quickly as possible. He found his jeans on the bed along with his shirt. It didn't take long for him to dress and gather up all the items he'd brought with him.

The shouting in the kitchen grew from muffled voices to painfully clear ones. He decided it might be wise to allow Freddie to deal with his fathers alone. His presence would only exacerbate the situation.

"Freddie?" Taine waved the younger man over. "Give me a call in the morning, all right?"

"Yeah."

Taine stepped out of the flat and stood staring out at the early morning sky. *"Bollocks."*

CHAPTER TWENTY-SEVEN

FREDDIE

The door closed on Taine. Freddie stared at it for a while. He brought his fist up to pound on it in annoyance.

"Freddie, *caru*?" His tad rushed over to drag him away from the front door before he injured himself. "Why don't we sit and have a nice little chat, hmm? Your dad can make tea."

"Sod your tea."

"Watch your language." His dad poked his head out of the kitchen to admonish him. "We'll talk like civilised individuals."

"Oh? Like you were civilised to Taine? You called him a paedophile." Freddie covered his face with his hands. "Oh God. I can't believe you said *that* to him. What's he going to think? What if he doesn't want to see me again?"

"Good."

Freddie shoved his tad away from him to move towards the kitchen. He'd never been so angry with either of his parents—*ever.* "No, not good. I *like* him. Do you hear me? I actually like him. What have you done? You've gone and called him a child molester. I'm not a child or even a teenager. I'm twenty-six years old. When are you going to treat me like an adult? I had to move into a completely different city *just* to have some sort of life. And you… you come here and you ruin it. Why would you do that?"

"Let's all calm down and talk this through." His tad held a hand out towards him and one towards his dad, ever the calm negotiator of peace.

"No, I think—" Freddie cut himself off. He steeled his nerves for what needed to be said. "I think you should both go home to the farm."

"Freddie?"

"Just go, please?" He didn't want to ruin his relationship with his fathers, but what had been said to Taine was almost unforgivable. "You called an honourable, kind, good man something truly disgusting. I can't deal with you both right now, not without saying something I'll regret."

Sitting on his couch with his head bowed, Freddie refused to look at his fathers. They left after several failed attempts to get him to speak. Both men stooped to kiss the top of his head on the way out.

Taine's never going to want to see me again.
Why would he?
The bitter thoughts filled Freddie's mind. He stamped

down the guilt at kicking his dads out, unable to shake the feeling that they'd cost him something—someone—who might have become important in his life.

By the time the sun came up and his alarm in the bedroom went off, Freddie hadn't moved an inch. He also hadn't gotten a minute of sleep. Work would be awful, but dealing with ill patients might put his life in perspective.

Always does.

Three cups of the strongest coffee at the hospital hadn't improved his mood. Neither did the text from his auntie suggesting he forgive his fathers for being "daft morons." Given what the loud silence from Taine might mean, mercy wasn't high on his list of things to do for the day.

"All right, I can't take it. You went on holiday. You should've come back relaxed. Instead, you're moping around my ward." Genevieve dropped into the chair across from him in his small office. "What went wrong?"

"My dads showed up last night." Freddie sipped mournfully at his coffee. "Taine and I were sharing a trifle in the kitchen—in our pants."

"They didn't." Gen sounded as horrified as he felt. "You weren't."

"They did. We were," he groaned succinctly.

It started with a muffled snort. Freddie glared at the normally composed doctor across from him. She choked on a giggle before bursting into laughter.

"Oh God, oh God." Gen tried to calm herself down without success.

"It's *not* funny." Freddie tried to maintain a stern scowl, but his lips quivered without his permission. He coughed and giggled at the same time. "Oh, Gen, you should've seen their faces when they saw Taine in his boxers, calmly eating custard. It's worse than the time they walked in on me wanking in my room."

Their eyes met. *Silence.* Both doctor and nurse ended up sliding out of their chairs to the floor, laughing until their lungs begged for air. He finally forced himself to keep his gaze away from her to regain control.

They needed another five minutes to be able to drag themselves up to their seats. Freddie tossed her one of the spare handkerchiefs in his desk drawer. He always kept them for clients.

"And Taine? How's he feel about all of this?" Gen asked the question he'd been avoiding. "Freddie?"

"No idea." He shrugged. "I haven't heard a peep out of him since last night."

"Call him." She nudged the desk phone with her ever-present cup of tea. "What? Why not? You can't be blamed for your dads being dads."

"Overprotective prats is what they are. And how could he not blame me?" Freddie scrubbed his fingers across his face. "They made a brilliant night beyond awkward. How do I apologise for it? I don't even know where to start."

"You have *nothing* to apologise for—if he can't see that, then he's not worth it." Gen shifted forward in her seat, resting both elbows on the edge of the desk. "What are you worried about?"

Freddie dropped his hands away when she pulled at them.

"He voiced concerns about being older than me. I never cared about the age difference, but how could this not affect him? The way my dads reacted will only feed into his own doubt. We've only just started to date—emotions aren't involved yet. Maybe he'll think a clean break is best?"

It sounded weak even to his own ears.

Gen smiled sadly at him. "Too early for emotions to be involved?"

"Of course," Freddie snapped defensively. He crossed his arms over his chest only to drop them when he realised how his body language proved her right. "*Coc y gath.*"

The day passed relatively quietly. Freddie didn't have any house visits to make this week. All of his work focused on organising schedules out through November and December; the end of the year tended to speed up and slow down almost in equal measures.

Several of the doctors stopped in to see him on their way out. Freddie had no desire to return home. His bed still smelled of Taine, who hadn't called—or answered his text.

"Freddie?"

He closed his eyes and dropped his head on the files spread in front of him on his desk. "Yes, Auntie Anna? You're a long way from home."

"I'm an hour from home. It's hardly the arctic circle." She waltzed into his office with her bright plum coat and a paper bag in her hand. "Up you get. I've exactly what you need."

"The dads' heads on a platter?"

"Maybe next year, love." Auntie Anna had always taken his side—almost always. She had a slightly clearer head than her brother and brother-in-law tended to have when it came to their beloved only child. "Now, what's this I hear about you being corrupted by an old man?"

"He's in his forties—not a hundred and forty." Freddie peeked into the bag to find she'd brought him several slices of her famous bara brith. He immediately grasped a slice to begin eating it; lunch had been ages ago. "I shouted at them."

"So I heard."

"Actually. Shouted." He couldn't quite believe he'd done it. "Should I feel guilty?"

"No, but I imagine you do anyway, which is why I came to visit." She pulled a thermos out of her large purse and set it on the desk. "Some of my spiced tea to cheer you up. We'll have tea and cake while you tell me all about your new man, who is apparently very fit."

"He is." Freddie couldn't help the slight dreaminess in his voice. His mind had immediately jumped back to when he'd seen Taine completely naked for the first time. "Incredibly fit."

"Eat up, and we'll figure out how to sort your dense dads out."

They didn't sort anything out. Freddie enjoyed six slices of bara brith and half the thermos of tea. His mood did improve, so the visit hadn't been a wasted one for his aunt.

With a promise to wring her brother's neck, his aunt had swanned off home. Freddie stayed in his office for another hour. His flat had zero attraction for him at the moment.

Go home. Nothing's going to get better by moping at the hospital.

CHAPTER TWENTY-EIGHT

TAINE
DECEMBER 24

At three in the morning on the twenty-fourth of December, Taine had been lying in bed attempting to convince himself to stop thinking about Freddie. He'd driven out a few days earlier to spend Christmas with Father Wilson. The Christmas Eve Mass at midnight extended until they'd returned to the house at half past two.

In the two months or more since the evening at Freddie's flat, no less than five people had ripped him a new one for abandoning the nurse without bothering to call or text him. Taine had meant to reach out to him. He had.

Yet, I haven't.

Remi suggested that perhaps since retiring from rugby,

the great Tens had lost his nerve. Scottie asked for Freddie's number. Caddock, Graham, and Dr Williams all lectured him on several occasions for making their happy bunny friend sad.

Bollocks.

I'm an arse.

A cowardly tosser of an arse.

Is that physically possible?

"Andrew?" Father Wilson knocked on the door before opening it. He held out a set of keys. "You'll be needing these, won't you? I'll pray for your safe journey to see your young man."

"Father?" Taine sat up and swung his legs around to sit up. "I'm here for Christmas."

"You've spent three days wandering about lost in your thoughts." He sat on the mattress, patting his adopted son on the knee. "Your friend Remi gave me a ring yesterday morning. He told me about this nurse, Freddie. For most of your life, I've been proud of how generous in spirit you are towards others. It's unlike you to simply never contact someone again. You like him."

"He's young."

"You're young." His aged hand on Taine's knee tightened with surprising strength. "What do you have to lose by spending time with this Freddie? You might not have talked about him, but you've had him in your thoughts since the night you walked out of his flat."

"Are you sure you were called to be a priest?" Taine asked tiredly. "It's twelve hours to Cornwall if I don't hit traffic and I don't stop for the loo more than a couple times."

"Well, you'll be there in time for Christmas supper." Father Wilson pushed himself up with help from Taine. "I'll prepare a basket of some of the cheese and shortbread the ladies brought last night. You shouldn't show up uninvited without bringing a gift."

He'd been on the road for an hour when his brain eventually caught up with what had happened. Father Wilson had not only approved of his choice of a much younger man, but had actively encouraged him to show up on Christmas to see him. He could only hope the door wouldn't be slammed in his face.

When Freddie's dad had lit into him, Taine's initial reaction had honestly been to put him on the ground. He wouldn't usually allow anyone to get away with calling him a paedophile. But a confrontation with the parents of a lover could have no winners, not really, so he left to avoid creating further drama.

He wouldn't apologise for leaving. Given all the options, it had been the wisest move to make. Freddie could handle his dads—they weren't abusive, just misguided.

The mistake he actually intended to apologise for was what happened next. *I should've called him, or texted, or better still, gone to see him at the hospital.* They'd shared a brilliant holiday and had sexually connected on a deep level, after all.

Halfway through the journey, his phone beeped with a message. He ignored it. *Safe driving, that's me.* It continued to go off periodically until the person finally called him instead of texting.

He hit the speakerphone button. "*What?*"

"Well, morning to you, Tens." Scottie sounded halfway to

drunk at ten after nine. "Been to church yet?"

"I'm not in Scotland."

"Why aren't you in Scotland?" Scottie suddenly appeared less boozed up, never a good sign. "You're going to Cornwall, aren't you? To see the bunny."

"Why are you calling me?"

"I was going to tell you to stop being a daft twat and find your bollocks long enough to call the bunny." He paused to clear his throat loudly and nauseatingly. "Seems I don't have to. Drive safe."

"Don't call—"

A sudden beep told him not to bother asking Scottie not to tell the others. He'd already hung up. No doubt to immediately begin gossiping with all their friends, who would be calling him to take the mickey soon enough.

Bollocks.

The constant calls did make the remaining seven hours of the drive go by faster. His GPS led him straight to the long drive into the Whittle family farm. He sat in the car, staring at the house all decked out in white and blue lights.

He wondered idly if the family celebrated both Hanukkah and Christmas. It would've made for loads of presents in December. *And now I'm trying to prolong the agony. Is Remi right? Have I lost my nerve?*

"Are you lost, love?"

Taine blinked several times to find a woman who had the same hair and eyes as Freddie climbing into the vehicle with him. "Not lost."

"You sure? You must've been lost to ignore our Freddie for two months." She smiled at him, and her smile reminded him of her nephew as well. "I'm sorry my brother and his husband lost their minds. It's stupid of them. They've struggled with seeing their son as an adult. I think you owe Freddie an apology."

Taine could only nod his agreement. "I'm aware."

"Well, good then, we'll get along brilliantly. C'mon. Let's get inside before the snow starts." She peered out the windscreen at the ever-darkening skies. "Well? What are you waiting for? You've had a long drive, I'd imagine."

He found himself bundled into the house with the basket from Father Wilson clutched in his arms. Freddie and his fathers were all seated in the den by the fireplace, watching *Doctor Who*. It appeared to be a family favourite from the rapt attention they were paying to the telly.

"Lads? You've a visitor."

Freddie glanced idly over his shoulder and froze in place. One of his fathers, Adam, reached out to grab the arm of his other dad to keep him from moving off the couch. Given the last time they met, it might've been a wise decision.

"Happy Christmas." Taine held out the basket in the general direction of all three Whittle men. "Hope I'm not interrupting."

"You are—" Fred Whittle trailed off when his husband elbowed him hard in the stomach. "You are most welcome."

Freddie grinned brightly at his fathers before turning to scowl at Taine. "Did you lose my number?"

"Excellent question, *cariad*," Fred interjected.

"You started the mess, so keep out of it this time." Freddie turned his narrowed eyes on his fathers. He stood up and waved for Taine to follow him. "Let's go see if it's snowing."

It was snowing, freezing cold as well. Freddie shoved his hands into his pockets and stamped his feet on the ground a few times. Taine didn't know if an offer of body warmth would be welcome at the moment.

"I'm sorry." Taine decided to get the easy words out of the way first. "I'm sorry for not calling or texting for two months."

"Not for leaving in the middle of the night?"

Taine shoved his own hands into his coat pockets. "No, we haven't known each other long enough for it to be wise for me to get between you and your fathers. Also, it was good for them to see you stand up for yourself."

"True." Freddie paced a small circuit in front of him. "It's freezing out here, but if we go inside, they'll eavesdrop on us."

He nodded his head towards the faces pressed against the kitchen window. "They're trying anyway."

Freddie strode away from the house towards a barn in the distance. "C'mon, it's warmer in here anyway."

They stood awkwardly in the only mildly warmer barn, staring at bales of hay. Taine didn't regret coming. He wished they could skip past the initial conversation, but knew he only had himself to blame.

"Would a text have killed you?" Freddie hopped up on one of the bales. His legs swung back and forth. "I mean, really, you could've called me."

"I'm sorry." Taine strode forward until he was within kicking distance. "I am so sorry, not for leaving but for allowing my doubts about age differences to cloud my judgement.

I missed you. Thought about you."

"Not enough to text?"

Taine gripped him by the knees, spread his legs, and stepped forward between them. "Forgive me, Frederick?"

"Why?"

"Because you missed me?"

Freddie tilted his head back to glare up at him. "Try again."

"Because I missed you?" Taine worked his hands further up the younger man's legs to massage his thighs gently. "Will you forgive me? I'll make it up to you."

Freddie's lips twitched slightly and then pressed tightly together. "Are you staying for supper?"

"I'll be buried in the pasture if I say no." Taine could well imagine the Whittle family coming together to punish him for hurting their Freddie. "I'd rather be buried in you."

Freddie snorted loudly and leaned forward until his head rested against Taine's jacket. "I did miss you. Why didn't you text?"

"I'm an arse."

"True." He wound his arms around Taine's waist. "I only started talking to my fathers at the beginning of December. It took them that long to admit they were wrong."

They stayed in the barn for several minutes—hugging. None of his friends would ever believe he'd spent time cuddling in a farm building with hay and animals. Freddie called it a *cwtch* and told him to shift closer.

The atmosphere in the house hadn't warmed any. It became clear that Adam and Anna had told off Fred while they were outside. The three sat, avoiding each other, pretending not to notice Freddie and Taine's return.

Freddie veered off from the living room to find the basket Taine brought with him. He peeked inside it and immediately came out with one of the items. "You brought cheese."

Taine chuckled at the enthusiastic shout from the younger man. "Happy Christmas."

CHAPTER TWENTY-NINE

FREDDIE

If Freddie had believed in Father Christmas, he might've asked for Taine to appear like an angel from Heaven at the farm. He didn't, so he hadn't. Yet the man had shown up out of the blue with a basket of Scottish treats.

There appeared to be several types of cheese in the basket. The Inverloch, in particular, excited the food-obsessed part of him. He batted away his aunt's hands when she tried to grab it off him.

"My cheese."

"Share the wealth, Freddie." She darted in to grab one of the rounds of cheddar. "Are you sure it's wise to leave him alone in the den with both of your fathers?"

"I'm making tea," Freddie muttered obstinately.

"Might help if you turn the kettle on, love." She patted his shoulder and waltzed out with her prize in hand. "I'll ensure no one actually ends up bloody and beaten."

He decided not to begrudge her the cheese if she managed to keep the three men in the living room from ending up brawling by the fire. "Good luck."

"Make the tea."

"I'm making the sodding tea." Freddie grabbed the kettle to fill it. "*Make the tea.*"

While staring at the bright red kettle, Freddie tried to mentally process the surprisingly immediate answer to his Christmas wish. The first month after the debacle at his flat with no contact from Taine had left him rather depressed. By the first of December, his Welsh common sense kicked him in the arse.

He had forced himself to ask a serious set of questions designed to add a dash of realism to the situation. Did he miss Taine? *Of course.* Had they been forging a deeper connection? *Certainly.* Were they in love? *Obviously not, we only met in July.* Would it be the end of the world if he never met the man again? *Sad, but not quite apocalyptic.*

With the injection of clear thinking, Freddie managed to pick himself up out of the haze of moping around. Gen, Graham, and BC had gotten together to take him out dancing a few times. They'd been joined by other friends of the rugby player as well.

He still didn't like Scottie, who seemed to enjoy his front of arsehole a bit too much.

All in all, December proved far better than November.

Standing up to his fathers had improved their relationship overall. The punk twits who harassed him had been forced out of the neighbourhood. Freddie now had friends—many of them.

What Freddie had missed most about Taine was the potential. The hints at the depths a relationship between them might have reached. He hoped this sudden Christmas appearance boded well for them.

With a tray loaded with tea, shortbread, and some of his aunt's bara brith, he headed towards the suspiciously quiet den. The separation between the four and the awkward silence reminded him of the few times when he was young that the Protestant and Jewish sides of their family came together during the holidays. He hesitated by the coffee table, trying to decide how best to resolve the situation.

Setting the tray down on the table, Freddie folded his arms across his chest and tilted his head to the side while narrowing his eyes on his fathers. Auntie Anna appeared to be trying to engage Taine in conversation. He didn't need three guesses to figure out why the attempts kept failing.

I will not spend my favourite day of the year with two sulking fathers, an uneasy potential boyfriend, and a grinning aunt.

I won't.

Freddie grabbed two pieces of shortbread before twisting around to fall lightly into Taine's lap. He handed one of the biscuits to the man with an innocent grin. "Happy Christmas. *Chag Sameach!*"

"Pardon?"

"Happy Holiday in Hebrew." Freddie munched on his shortbread. It fell apart in his mouth, beautifully buttery with a hint of sugar and lemon. "Did your priest make this?"

"Aye." Taine raised an eyebrow sardonically at him. He could clearly see what Freddie intended to do with his somewhat provocative actions. "Father Wilson believes one should never show up as a guest without bringing gifts."

"Are you Catholic?"

Freddie's eyes snapped towards his tad. "Hasn't our family endured enough religious conflict to not drag someone else into it?"

"Why don't we all have tea?" Anna interjected into the conversation, deflecting whatever response his fathers would've thrown out. "Tea, bread, and biscuits. Isn't there *Doctor Who* to watch?"

"I'm more interested in why our Christmas has been invaded." His dad held his hand up to stop both Freddie and his aunt from starting in on him. "He obviously upset you, whether we created the initial drama or not. Now he's waltzing in with cheese and biscuits. It's within our right to ask what he's about."

"No, it's not." Freddie brushed his crumb-covered fingers on his trousers. "It's mine."

"He—"

"*Adam*," Anna snapped at her brother. "Eat some bara brith."

Freddie realised that, despite their promises, his fathers still struggled with the idea of their son being an adult. "BC invited me over to the inn for a holiday party. I think I'll take him up on the offer. Taine? Want to join me?"

Without saying another word, Freddie stood to head for the door. On Christmas, his favourite day of the year, he absolutely refused to engage in an argument with his family. Perhaps, if left to their own devices, they might manage to realise how serious the situation had become.

His life couldn't revolve around helping his fathers stay in their comfort zone. Freddie wondered if living at home into his twenties hadn't exacerbated the situation. He should've moved out years earlier than he had.

Grabbing the basket from the kitchen and his coat from the door, Freddie stormed out of the house. He paused in the yard, trying to decide how to get the Mini out from where the other vehicles had blocked it in. Taine stepped up beside him and dropped a heavy arm across his shoulders.

"How about we go in mine?" Taine would likely fit better in his Bentley than in the much smaller Mini. Freddie gave a mental snicker at the six-foot-five man squashing into his car. "You sure you want to go?"

Freddie glanced over his shoulder to peer into one of the windows. He could see his aunt standing over his fathers with her hands on her hips. Auntie Anna tended to give rather long and loud lectures. *"Definitely."*

Riding in the luxurious Bentley Falcon distracted him for the first bit of the thirty-minute drive to the inn. Freddie grabbed his mobile to text Graham. He didn't want their arrival to be a surprise.

"You realise you've given them a head start to think of jokes to torture us with when we arrive." Taine reached down to turn up the heat. "Are you warm enough?"

"Toasty." Freddie had plenty of room to stretch out his legs. He resisted the urge to lower the window to stick his hand out to catch some of the falling snow. "I love this time of year, even if it's too cold to want to do anything outside."

"Thought you hated being cold?"

"I do." Freddie waved his hand absently to his knit hat, scarf, gloves, and multiple layers. "If I added any more clothes, I'd be waddling around instead of walking."

Taine moved his hand from the gear lever to Freddie's knee. He gave it a squeeze. "I've missed you."

He canted his head to the side. "Have you? You could've easily solved the problem by picking up your phone."

"Touché." Taine left his hand on Freddie's knee. "Forgive me for being an idiotic twat? Scottie's words, not mine."

Freddie covered the hand on his leg. "Don't be a twat again."

"I'll do my best."

CHAPTER THIRTY

TAINE

Pulling up the drive to the inn, Taine realised with a sense of dread that all of their friends had gathered for Christmas. He recognised the collection of vehicles parked outside of it. *Bollocks.* Given how much they'd all harassed him to contact Freddie, he had no doubt the entire group would be insufferable.

The inn had been completely decked out for Christmas, both inside and out. A smug, grinning BC and Caddock stood on the steps waiting for them. *Shite.* He would rather have faced Remi or the foul-mouthed Scottie.

"Happy Christmas." Caddock waltzed over to take Freddie by the arm and lead him into the inn. "Don't take long, BC, we want Tens mostly unfrozen."

Taine watched the Brute swan off with Freddie. "What won't take long?"

BC glared at him with all the ferocity that he'd used to stare at their opponents on the rugby pitch. It might've worked if he hadn't been wearing a cardigan with a reindeer on it. "The nurse is a nice kid."

"The nurse has a name." Taine made a show of perusing the cardigan. "Does the reindeer have one? Is it perhaps ugly?"

"We like Freddie." BC strode down the steps towards Taine. "Not sure how I feel about you at the moment. Who ignores someone they just buggered for over two months?"

"Almost every friend of ours at least three times over the course of our sex lives?" Taine pulled his mobile out of his pocket. "Would you like me to list your own alphabetically?"

"Never texting you again."

"Liar." He walked around the man to head up the stairs towards the inn. "Why *exactly* did you waylay me?"

BC adjusted his cardigan and shrugged. "Graham thought I should be the one to impress the importance of you not acting like a fuckwit again."

"Duly noted."

He threw an arm around Taine's shoulder. "Rupert brought every type of beer he could find. Bet you a hundred quid at least one of us runs starkers on the beach by the end of the day."

"Nothing says Christmas like frozen bollocks and public indecency." Taine remembered several other occasions in their long history as friends that had ended similarly. "Put my money on Scottie."

"Cheater."

The two laughed their way through the inn until they found everyone in the library. Taine caught the beer tossed across the room. Even if his friends thought he'd been an arse, the atmosphere felt overwhelmingly welcoming compared to what had happened at the Whittle farm.

Over food Mrs Morgan had prepared for all of them, everyone shared their nightmare stories of holidays with the family. They universally agreed the Hodson twins, Rupert and Graham, had the best of the worst. Their mother had forced them into matching elf costumes one year—they'd been fourteen.

Francis had photos—ones that Graham in particular fought to throw into the fire.

Taine sank into one of the larger armchairs. He tossed an arm out to grab Freddie when he wandered past. They *both* studiously ignored the wolf whistles around the room.

"We should snog," Freddie remarked casually. "They're all far too interested in me sitting in your lap."

"Snogging won't help." Taine grabbed a pillow to wing at Scottie, who'd started making kissy faces at him. *Arse.* "Is this how we're spending Christmas? Shit beer and appetisers?"

Pushing Freddie out of his lap, Taine led the younger man out of the room. He caught his hand to guide him out the back door and into the brisk night air. The snow had picked up considerably in the past hour.

Freddie raced out into the winter storm. He twirled around with his head tilted up towards the sky. "Hate the cold. Love snow."

"Snow is cold," Taine pointed out helpfully. "I believe it's one of the requirements in the making of it."

"Don't be difficult. I've only just forgiven you." Freddie grabbed a handful of snow to fling into his face. "We could slow dance."

"In the snow?" He didn't think it would be the safest decision to dance around on a slick and icy surface. "Now? With drunken friends watching and ready to mock me for it?"

"Yes."

They danced slowly, slipping and sliding on the frozen ground. No music aside from the wind, ocean, and rambunctious twits inside the inn. Taine's arms wound tightly around Freddie, mostly to conserve warmth, while the brisk night air cut through them.

"We've an audience." Freddie gestured behind them. "In the windows."

Taine rolled his eyes but chuckled at his friends. The lot of them had written numbers on cards to score their dancing. "We've averaged a seven out of ten."

Freddie leaned up on his tiptoes with his cold fingers sliding around Taine's neck. Their lips brushed together. "This seemed far more romantic in the movies."

"What movie?"

"Don't remember. It had cheese in it."

"In a romantic movie? You remember the dancing in the snow and the cheese?" Taine pulled his head back with his arms still around the younger man. "Are you sure it wasn't a dream?"

"I have a present for you." Freddie ignored his question

and drifted out of his arms to trudge up the hill. "It's rather small."

"Is it cheese?"

He kicked snow at Taine in response. "No, though I could give you some if you like."

"What's this present?"

Freddie eased a velvet bag out of his pocket and tilted the contents into Taine's hand when he held it out. "It's jade. Graham has a friend who travelled to New Zealand recently. The design is traditional. It's called a *manaia* carving? I think he said. It's supposed to signify a connection to the Maori—to New Zealand—and also protection."

Taine clutched the carved jade symbol in his icy fingers, careful not to crush it. He'd read about the *manaia,* a mythological creature in the Maori culture often shown as part man and part animal. The one Freddie had gifted him with happened to have the body of a human and the head of a serpent. The pendant hung from a thick leather cord.

The gift touched him deeply. Aside from his adoptive father, no one usually acknowledged his dual heritage. He barely did himself.

"I… thank you." Taine couldn't take his eyes off the dark green carving in his hand.

"You're wel—"

Taine threw his worries over their audience to the brisk wind. He caught Freddie by the hair to drag him into his arms, cool shivering lips crashing against one another. The kiss would doubtlessly leave them breathless with swollen lips and demonstrate his appreciation for it. "Thank you."

Freddie grinned broadly at him, licking his lips. "Happy Christmas, Taine."

"Happy Christmas, Frederick."

"Oi! Love-twats, get your arses inside before you turn into popsicles," Scottie yelled from an open window. "BC's opening the whisky. Since Francis and Caddock left, we can finally have a decent-sized drink."

"You've got some genuinely classy friends." Freddie shivered when the wind picked up. "Whisky does sound brilliant."

Taine twisted around to start down the hill only to lose his footing and slide on his arse through the snow. "*Bollocks.*"

"Frozen ones, I'd imagine." Freddie crouched beside him. "Let's get inside before you break something. Old people are so fragile."

"*Arse.*"

CHAPTER THIRTY-ONE

FREDDIE

Morning dawned rather bright and early for all the residents at the Fisherman's Refuge. Freddie woke up to find himself on the floor, squashed under a table with Taine to his left and a stack of marmite toast on his right. The smell of the spread didn't do much for his stomach.

Twisting around on his back, Freddie winced when his shoulder whacked into the solid wooden leg. He stretched out his legs only to kick over several bottles. The sound woke Taine, who shot up only to smash into the underside of the table.

"Well, if the hangover didn't give you a headache, the concussion will." Freddie grabbed one of the slices of bread to offer to the groaning man beside him. "Marmite toast?"

"Is it torture Taine day?" Taine attempted to avoid the bread only to catch himself on the other table legs. "What the bloody hell are we doing under the dining room table?"

"Not a clue." He crawled out from under it, avoiding the toast and bottles. "Mrs Morgan's going to beat us all with a wooden spoon. We've made quite a mess."

"Why is there marmite toast?" Taine clambered out with one hand rubbing the back of his head. He kicked at an empty jar of the stuff on the floor. "What in the world did we do last night?"

"Toast and bowling with beer bottles?" Freddie hazarded a guess from the position of the bottles and a rugby ball nearby. "Maybe the toast was for the winners?"

"Or losers?"

Stumbling into one of the chairs not overturned, Freddie gently massaged his aching head. He couldn't recall ever being quite so pained after a night of drinking. His evenings at the pub were usually restricted to one or two pints of beer.

His stomach rolled uneasily. *How much did we drink last night?* There would be a number of sore heads when everyone else woke up.

The nurse in him decided it might be best to prepare for the inevitable. His auntie Anna had always sworn by lots of water, orange juice, and bananas to fight off the ill stomach and headache. He'd never had to test it out himself.

Better make sure Taine hasn't actually gotten a concussion from bashing his skull into the table.

Given the signs of one might coincide a bit with symptoms of drinking far too much the previous night, Freddie opted to check Taine's eyes. His pupils seemed fine, not overly dilated. He managed to track the finger moving in front of him fine, as well.

He had a bit of a lump on his head, but nothing massive. No trouble with his vision, no numbness or tingling, he didn't appear dazed or confused. His headache and nausea likely came from alcohol more than anything else.

Satisfied with the results of his impromptu examination, Freddie left Taine to make his way into the kitchen. Mrs Morgan had left them with plenty of scones, saffron buns, and other baked goods. He found a bit of fruit in the fridge, along with juice.

"Playing housekeeper?"

Freddie paused in the middle of pouring a cup of juice for himself. He stared in amazement at the figure in the doorway. Scottie wore pink pants and a Santa hat. "Merry Christmas?"

"Some shit stole my clothes." Scottie slurred half his words, obviously still well into his cups. "All of them."

"But you found pink pants and a Santa hat?" Freddie turned on the coffee machine. He thought several of them might need to sober up a bit before curing their hangovers. "Dare I ask where you found them?"

"In my room."

"Someone stole your clothes and left you pink pants and a Santa hat?"

"Could you stop fucking saying it? It hasn't fucking changed." Scottie advanced into the kitchen. He would've been intimidating—except for his new lacy pants. "Have you made coffee? Why are you awake and in the fucking kitchen?"

If Scottie wore regular clothes, Freddie might've found his hulking approach a bit terrifying. He never found out what the mostly naked man intended to say. The sauced rugby player stumbled from the kitchen, muttering to himself about evil elves snatching his trousers.

Pots of tea and coffee sat on the counter by the time a showered and changed Taine joined him. Freddie hopped up beside his own mug of coffee and pulled out his mobile when it buzzed. His aunt apparently applauded his staying away, but thought a Boxing Day brunch might give his dads a chance at redemption.

Freddie: Not sure brunch is our wisest plan ever.

Anna: Afraid of their reaction? Or did you lot get a bit drunk last night? I heard from Mrs Morgan this morning. Did things get loud?

Freddie: A bit.

Anna: Tea then. You can't put the issue off forever, nor can you run away every time they do something idiotic. We'll have tea. They love you enough to listen.

Love, Freddie thought, had never been the issue. Until his fathers accepted their son as an adult, nothing would ever change. They'd continue to bash their heads together, no matter who he dated.

Sipping the coffee he'd fixed for himself, Freddie pondered the invitation to tea. What was that quote about insanity from Albert Einstein? He vaguely remembered one of his university professors repeating it constantly during one of his lessons.

Insanity: doing the same thing over and over again and expecting different results.

How many times should he place his heart into a bear trap and hope not to have it smashed to bits? For his beloved fathers? He probably ought to do it at least one more time. What harm could tea do? If his aunt had her way, the two men would be on their best behaviour.

He side-eyed Taine, who stood next to him, staring blankly into his own coffee. "Have any plans for this afternoon?"

Taine lifted his head slowly, as if he had to move it through treacle. "I barely made it through a shower. Why?"

"How do you feel about tea?"

"I'm drinking coffee." Taine was either still drunk or not completely awake. "Think it's coffee. Is it coffee?"

"Definitely." Freddie couldn't help a snicker at him with his bleary eyes. "Want to go for tea later?"

Taine blinked. *Twice.* "Sure."

"Wonderful." Freddie eased off the counter and chugged down the last of his coffee. "I'll get in the shower. Hope the elves left my trousers alone."

He made it halfway down the hall before Taine's groggy voice followed him from the kitchen. "Did you say elves?

CHAPTER THIRTY-TWO

TAINE

When coffee didn't help get his mind in gear, Taine wandered out into the freezing weather. He let the bracing wind wake him up. With a clearer head, it occurred to him that tea probably wasn't *just* tea.

Bollocks.

He had managed to hold his anger by the skin of his teeth at the Whittle farm. Another extended afternoon with Freddie's fathers might be more than his slow-to-rise temper could handle. He wondered if perhaps he had gotten far more attached than he was ready to admit.

He walked up the hill, managing it better than the previous night. His breath puffed out in front of him with each exhale. *What am I doing? Aside from freezing my arse off.*

The Cornish coast shone in the winter sunlight. It almost tempted him to walk the path down the beach itself. He couldn't help enjoying clear skies—despite the beyond freezing temperatures.

"Tenner for your thoughts?"

Taine waited until Caddock had joined him at the top of the bluff. "How's Francis? Did the beer bother him last night?"

His old teammate's husband tended to suffer panic attacks around drunks, for good reason as he'd been attacked twice by drunken men. They tried to respect his wishes. None of them had been surprised when the married couple left for Looe before they broke into the heavier liquor.

"His granny's a bit under the weather, so he stayed home." Caddock didn't bother to answer the question, which hopefully meant Francis hadn't been overly bothered. "Is there a reason you're doing your best impression of Jack Frost?"

"Curing my hangover."

"By icing your brain?" Caddock shivered beside him. "Have you made up with your nurse?"

"He's not *mine*."

"Lying to yourself is pathetic." He punched Taine hard on the arm. "Look, remember after my brother died, you pulled me aside and gave me the kick in the arse I needed to look after my little nephew properly?"

"Of course I remember. You stopped talking to me for months." Taine hadn't actually heard from Caddock until a week before his wedding. "What does that have to do with anything?"

"As Francis would say, you've a lovely young man in

Freddie. And as I would say, stop acting like a sodding idiotic prat. I thought we designated Scottie as the group moron." He nudged him with his elbow. "Freddie's a good lad. He's sweet. He's halfway to falling in love with you and has no idea, so don't bollocks it up any more than you already have."

"Caddock." Taine rubbed his temples firmly, trying to soothe the sudden return of his headache. "He can't possibly be falling in love with me. It's too soon."

"Maybe not there yet, but if you stopped trying to end things before they started, he'd bloody well be there." His friend sounded far too confident for Taine's mental stability. "Does Freddie know you had a word with your friend at Scotland Yard, who had a talk with his friend in Cardiff, who made sure the homophobic twats never step foot near him again? A lot of effort for someone you're done with."

"I never said I was *done* with him. When did I say that?" Taine whacked Caddock in the chest. "What exactly is the point of this conversation?"

"You did ignore him for two months." Caddock turned towards him, out of the wind that suddenly kicked up. "The point of the conversation is to ensure you maintain your reputation as the intelligent and thoughtful member of our little group of retirees. BC's too busy having a laugh, Remi's too French, and Scottie is—well—Scottie."

"And you?"

"I'm the Brute. No one's ever going to look at someone with a nickname like that and think, 'oh he's got a good head on his shoulders.' All I'm saying is, if the nurse is giving you a second chance, take it." Caddock grabbed him by the sleeve to tug him towards the inn. "It's sodding freezing out here. Let's get inside before we catch a cold."

"Catch a cold?" Taine couldn't help barking out a laugh at his old friend. "Marriage has changed you. Remember the time we all played naked rugby because we'd lost a bet to the Scottish national team?"

"I've expunged it from my memory."

"Definitely been around your husband too long." Taine rubbed his hands together in an attempt to warm them up. "I can't recall ever hearing you use a word like expunge."

"Oi. Have you seen my trousers?"

Taine glanced over at Scottie and quickly turned away. "I'd like to *expunge* that from my memory."

Flipping him off, Scottie shuffled down the hallway, obviously still hunting for his clothing. Taine chuckled with Caddock, who pointed towards a bag tucked into the rafters in the living room. *Idiots.* He should've known the Brute had been part of stealing their volatile friend's trousers.

"When are you going to put him out of his misery?" Taine hoped they'd return the clothes eventually. Scottie didn't tend to take jokes all that brilliantly. "He'll blow a gasket if you don't."

"It was BC's idea."

"Of course it was." He dragged his fingers through his hair roughly. "You don't think it might cause a fight?"

"Talk to BC." Caddock shrugged.

"I need more coffee." Taine left the idiots to their pranks and returned to the kitchen to see if anyone had refilled the kettle. Scottie would hit the roof when he found out. It was best to be completely prepared or out of range of his fists. "Right. Better find Freddie."

CHAPTER THIRTY-THREE

FREDDIE

Something had changed. He didn't know what or why, but Taine had been a bit different when Freddie returned to the kitchen, freshly showered, in his own trousers but with a borrowed T-shirt from Graham, who might've been smaller than the other blokes, yet the hem still hung down at Freddie's thighs.

Shaking his head to clear his ears of water, Freddie tried to observe the men crammed into the kitchen without overtly staring at them. Scottie hadn't surfaced from his room after locating his clothing. Freddie didn't think the temper tantrum had anything to do with it.

Something else has happened.

Why are they all surreptitiously looking between Taine

and me?

Caddock, in particular, appeared to smirk and mutter to BC whenever Taine glared at them. "Enjoy the shower?"

Freddie narrowed his eyes on the man. "Have I done something wrong? You're all rather carefully avoiding looking at me. It's unnerving. Stop it."

After a round of mumbled apologies, Freddie still knew nothing more about the *atmosphere* in the room. Taine merely shrugged when he raised an eyebrow at him in query. *Honestly.* They acted as if he'd caught them with their hands in the biscuit tin.

"All right, this is beyond ridiculous. I'm not enjoying my coffee with you *twmffats*." He grabbed his mug of fresh coffee and headed out of the room, rolling his eyes when muffled voices followed him. "I can hear you."

"Bollocks."

While in the shower, Freddie had taken the time to think through tea with the family. His aunt would consider it a test, another sign she watched far too much telly. The hot water had helped calm his nerves about it.

Finding the library empty, Freddie curled up in a weathered leather chair by the fire. He sipped his coffee and stared blankly at the flames. In the end, it all boiled down to what this holiday visit meant.

And what do I want it to mean?

"Sorry about the idiots." Taine joined him, practically collapsing into the chair across from him. He held out a saffron bun. "Want one? I managed to rescue it from the beasts in the kitchen who inhale anything in sight."

"What was it all about?" Freddie balanced his coffee on the arm of the chair. He enjoyed the warming scent of the fresh baked bun. "What happened?"

Taine shifted uneasily in his chair. His eyes glinted from the flickering flames with a fierce passion when he finally lifted his head to meet Freddie's eye. "I've a question to ask."

"I'm not marrying you."

"Well, good, I'm not asking. I've only known you since July." Taine smiled when Freddie grinned at him. "Irrepressible Frederick. I would like to date you."

"We've been dating."

"Exclusively." Taine scowled playfully at the interruption. "I want to be the only man in your life—romantically speaking."

"Anything else you'd like?"

His smile turned feral and wicked almost instantly. "I'm going to warm your arse with my hand and show you all the places a dominant man can take you."

"Right this second?" Freddie glanced from the coffee to the bun in his hand. "Snack first?"

"*Frederick.*"

"Yes?" He took a slow-motion bite from the saffron bun. "How can I help?"

"Don't be cheeky." Taine shifted forward in his chair and reached out to grip Freddie firmly by the knee. "Not opposed to dragging you across my knees here in the library where anyone could see or hear you."

Freddie chewed his bite of food methodically, eyes never wavering from Taine's. He twisted his lips up into a smile.

"Not sure your friends could survive the experience."

The air of the room seemed suddenly charged with heat that didn't come from the fireplace. Taine's hand weighed heavily on his leg. His hold tightened almost to the point of pain.

I've hit a trigger.

An honest to goodness trigger in the man.

I wonder how far I can make him jump with it.

With all the self-control learned in nursing school, Freddie kept his smile from widening visibly. In his twenty-plus years of life thus far, he never realised such a cheeky brat lay hidden in the depths of his personality. Taine brought out the best—or worst—in him, depending on one's perspective.

He stretched his legs out, crossing them at the ankles and forcing Taine's hand to shift. "You technically haven't asked a question. You said what you wanted."

"I did." Taine moved both of his hands to grab the legs of the chair to drag it closer. "Would you like to hear my question?"

Freddie had to work not to swallow his tongue when firm fingers worked their way up the inside of his thigh. "Aside from the one you just asked?"

Taine flicked the inside of Freddie's thigh, inches from his cock. "Are you going to submit to me?"

The word "submit" sent shivers up his spine. They caused him to twitch in his trousers, which in turn made Taine chuckle darkly. The sound only served to increase the sensation.

Oh God.

A laugh shouldn't have the power to set his entire body

on edge with arousal. Freddie couldn't maintain his mask of indifference. He didn't actually see the point when the evidence of his interest was outlined through his trousers.

"If you shag him in my library, you're paying to have the chairs cleaned," BC shouted on his way past the doorway. "And the walls, the whole sodding room."

"Would Graham mind if I shoved him off the cliff?" Taine remarked idly. He didn't move away or shift the chair, and his fingers continued on their path to trace the proof of Freddie's arousal. "Shall I take your cock doing an impression of carbon steel as a yes? Will you let me top you? Tie you up again? Show you the depths of my depravity? Drag you down with me and up to the highest levels of pleasure you've ever known?"

"Depths of your depravity?" Freddie tended to babble when he spoke. He didn't think his ramblings had ever sounded as pornographically arousing as Taine's did. "My answer is still yes."

Taine's lightly teasing fingers dropped down hard on his shaft. Freddie pressed his lips together to keep from an embarrassingly loud groan. The idea of others being around might be exhilarating, but the men would definitely take the mickey at every opportunity. He decided silence would be best.

"We have tea with my dads." Freddie went with the phrase most likely to dim the thickening atmosphere in the library. "Want to head to the farm early? I didn't get to show you around. You can see where we make the cheese. And the cows, we've lots of cows. There's a shed that's mine on the edge of the property."

"Why?"

"Because when I was learning to play the bagpipes, my dads almost lost their minds. They built me a little clubhouse to practice." Freddie had renovated the shed over the years. It looked less like the bright, cheery place of his youth and more grown-up. "It's brilliant."

"Is it?" Taine shifted back into his seat, hands disappointingly moving away from Freddie's body. "How big is this shed?"

"Why?" Freddie didn't know whether to be suspicious or excited about the sudden change in the man's tone of voice. "Do I want to know what you're thinking about? I don't. It's going to be brilliantly awful. The cows don't need to hear me shagging. It's going to be shagging, isn't it? Oh God."

Taine stood up, accidentally—though likely on purpose—brushing his own jean-covered cock across Freddie's face. "You'll find out eventually."

"*Cach.*"

"Up you get." Taine grabbed him by the shoulders to lift him easily up on his feet. "I want to see you play the bagpipes."

"Then I can play yours?"

"Something like that." Taine strode out of the room without giving him more of an answer. "You coming?"

"I hope so," Freddie muttered hopefully.

CHAPTER THIRTY-FOUR

TAINE

When Freddie mentioned playing the bagpipes, Taine hadn't quite believed him. He thought perhaps the man might be a bit of an armchair player. The last thing he expected was to sit on the scruffy couch in the shed and listen to him go through *Amazing Grace, Going Home,* and several other classic songs.

Taine applauded, honestly impressed, while Freddie carefully stowed his instrument in a wooden chest in the far corner of the room. "So, this is your childhood playhouse?"

Freddie grinned sheepishly. He wiped his hands on his trousers and glanced around the small shed. "I might've redecorated it a bit in my twenties."

"It's a brilliant place to hide." Taine hadn't known what to expect inside the garden variety shed, based on its outward appearance. "How much time did you spend out here as a lad?"

Freddie perched on the edge of the now closed wooden chest. "Hours. If I wasn't in the house, or on the farm, I was in here."

"No friends?"

"I had friends." Freddie didn't sound quite so confident. "A few. The cows. A few crows."

"Crows?"

"Crows are brilliant." He glared petulantly at Taine before the expression melted away into something that seemed melancholy. "I didn't quite fit in with most of the kids in my school. Too happy and hyper. Too Jewish. Too—so many things."

Taine could certainly relate to not being the average child's idea of normal. "Is this why you give far more than you should to your patients?"

"Pardon?" Freddie tilted his head to the side, as if trying to decipher what he meant. "I give them everything they deserve."

"Maybe." Taine stretched his legs out in the cramped space, unable to fully spread them out. "I wondered if maybe you offered them everything you didn't receive."

"Leave the psychoanalyzing to the professionals." Freddie lifted his legs up quickly to avoid Taine's kick. "If I'm compensating for anything, it would be all the family I've lost to cancer. Nothing feels more helpless as a child than watching someone you love fade away, never understanding why. Those deaths are what drive me to offer every bit of comfort and assistance that I possibly can."

It might be part of the truth, but Taine didn't believe it was all of it. He'd seen Freddie run himself ragged for his patients to the detriment of his own health.

Sitting in silence for several minutes, Taine considered the man seated across from him. They had a good thirty minutes or so to go before tea. *Whatever will we do with the time?* He found the idea of creating new memories with Freddie in his clubhouse thrilling.

"Do I want to know what you're thinking? I don't, do I? It's going to be something depraved and brilliant." Freddie's brown eyes brightened at whatever had sprung to his imagination. "You realise we can't appear too rumpled for tea. They'd know. Not the best of impressions. We want to de-escalate the situation, not make it worse. Also, I'm distinctly lacking in lube and condoms. Never was a scout—never prepared enough to be one."

"Freddie?" Taine waited until the rambling stopped short. "Breathe."

"Right. Breathing." Freddie inhaled deeply and exhaled slowly. "*Breathing.*"

Freddie did have one good point. They didn't have lubricant or condoms. Taine had explored the gamut of sex enough to know creative uses of other liquids in the place of lube usually ended messily and often painfully.

I thought I made a mental note to never think about that one time again.

Trying not to visibly shudder, Taine shoved the memory out of his mind. One of his early sexual experiences involved an experiment with using a heated pain-relieving cream. They did learn two important things: it burned like hell, and neither he nor his partner was a true sadist or masochist.

No amount of soaking in an ice bath had removed the burn entirely from either cock or arse. The suffering had lasted for several hours. It blissfully ended before a trip to the hospital became a necessity.

How the hell would we have explained ourselves?

"Taine?" Freddie tapped him on the knee with his knuckles. "What *are* you thinking about?"

"You," Taine lied easily before catching the younger man by the wrist to yank him across the shed. He twisted him around to lay him across his spread knees. His hand dropped on Freddie's trouser-covered arse. "Any ideas for how we can pass the time?"

Freddie wiggled across his legs. "Do you have any idea how painfully your muscles dig in to my ribs?"

"Budge up." Taine swatted pert cheek to encourage him. "There you go. Comfy?"

"Is anyone ever comfortable across someone's knees?" he asked rhetorically.

Wrapping one arm around Freddie's back to hold him in place, Taine deftly reached underneath to loosen his belt and unbutton his trousers. He easily slid them down to the younger man's ankles. His boxers stayed up to catch any potential mess.

Better his underwear than my trousers.

His fingers ran along several of the seams of the soft cotton boxers. Taine kept his initial touches light and gentle to balance against the periodic sharp swats. Balancing sweet pleasure with the hot heat of a good spanking required patience and concentration.

With Freddie situated in such a way that his thigh rubbed against Taine's shaft with any movement, patience and concentration didn't exactly come easily to him. He drew on all those years of experience on the rugby pitch that had ingrained perseverance in him. His fingers danced along the younger man's inner thigh.

"Oh. *Oh.*" Freddie groaned when Taine played a staccato beat against his arse. "What—"

In the general scheme of things, Taine thought talking incredibly overrated during sex. It meant nothing if Freddie was coherent enough to chatter. The younger man didn't manage much beyond groaning when blows of varying degrees landed on his behind.

It didn't take long for Freddie to begin grinding his already leaking cock against Taine's thigh. His boxers didn't, in the end, provide much of a barrier. Taine could feel the moisture starting to spread across his trousers.

Shite.

Might have trouble explaining that to his fathers.

Ah, sod it, not my problem.

Taine dipped into the top of Freddie's boxers. His index finger trailed along his crack, teasing the younger man's sensitive rosebud. He tugged his hand out to resume his experiment.

How pink will his bottom be by the time he's messed his boxers?

Or by the time I mess my own if he doesn't quit rubbing against my damn cock.

The wriggling in his lap worked on the tight grip Taine had over his iron will. Freddie seemed to shift more wildly with each swat. It was maddening—for both of them.

His hand hovered over Freddie's arse. He could feel the heat from the nurse's reddened cheeks against the palm of his hand, a heady and powerful sensation for anyone who had even the barest hint of a dominant streak in their personality.

He had caused the writhing. His swats turned the pale bottom into scorching-hot flesh. The growing damp spot on their clothes started with *him.*

True power.

True dominance.

It all starts and ends with fanning the blossoming flames of pleasure in a lover.

Taine wanted to set a fire off in Freddie so strong not even a twenty-foot tsunami could put it out. *All right, Afoa, a tad dramatic, reel yourself back a bit.* He meant it, though. In the deeper parts of his heart—the ones he usually ignored—he knew this could be different.

Would be.

I'm ready for different.

A grunt from Freddie brought his attention back to more pertinent matters, like the rock-hard evidence of their arousal. Taine lifted him up a little, so their cloth-covered shafts aligned better. They both exhaled almost in unison at the sudden contact.

Yanking down Freddie's boxers, so they rested just under

his bright red arse, Taine relished in the pleasure of the palm of his hand connecting with a bare cheek. The change in sound woke the beast in his blood. His teasing glances flowed readily into searing hits that bounced the younger man in his lap.

Their entire bodies froze each time their cocks crashed into one another. *Too much. Never enough.* Taine gripped Freddie firmly by the arse to guide his grinding. His fingers dug into the heated skin, adding enough of a flash of pain with the thrusting that it set the younger man off on a roller coaster of pleasure.

The moans from Freddie along with his out of control writhing had Taine going off in his own pants. He wilted into the couch cushions. It took several moments before he had the wherewithal to help his captive sit up more comfortably.

Freddie dropped onto the sofa beside him with a tired grunt. "*Cach.*"

"So, ready for tea?" Taine teased, still a little breathless. "You made a mess on my trousers. You should lick that up for me."

"*Twmffat.*"

CHAPTER THIRTY-FIVE

FREDDIE

After the heat had faded away, Freddie collected himself. He thought Taine seemed more centred somehow, but couldn't put his finger on why. It was a feeling he couldn't quite shake.

The thought slipped away from him when Freddie's eyes caught sight of the massive wet spot on Taine's trousers. *Cach.* He hoped the man kept a spare change of clothes in his vehicle. Tea would definitely devolve into a disaster if his dads caught sight of damp jeans.

And he won't exactly fit in mine, will he? Be like shoving too much meat in a sausage casing.

Thankfully for both their sakes, Taine's travel kit stashed in the rear of his Bentley hadn't been moved. While he switched out of his mucked-up trousers, Freddie dragged his own up.

He could run up to his old room for a fresh set of clothes without drawing too much unwanted attention.

The mood in the farmhouse didn't initially appear drastically changed from Christmas Day. His dads were edgy and tense. His aunt tried to counteract it by being overly jolly and trying to cheer everyone up, a trait he obviously inherited from her.

Dashing upstairs to his old bedroom, Freddie scrounged around for clean boxers, jeans, and a shirt of his own. A shower would've been nice, but it would've taken too long. He dragged a blue cardigan over his head; even with the fireplace, the old house could be cold in the winter.

He didn't want to leave Taine alone with his family for too long. It might traumatise the man. He might run away and never come back.

Hearing sounds in the kitchen, Freddie veered off the path to the den to help bring in the tea. His tad gave him a warm smile. They worked together to get everything sorted on two trays.

"Are you and Dad all right?" Freddie might've been frustrated with them, but he loved his fathers. "Did you have supper last night?"

His tad paused while pouring hot water into the teapot. "Realising our son is old enough to make his own choices has been sobering and difficult. We love you, *cariad*. We're proud of our baby boy. I know you're all grown up. It's just impossible to not see the little brown-haired lad who trotted around the farm in his Paddington wellies when I look at you. I'm sorry we hurt you, and so is your dad. It's the last thing we'd want to do."

Freddie threw his arm around the man, careful of the kettle in his hand. "Love you, Tad."

"We'll give your Taine a fair shake, *cariad*. I promise, both your dad and I will." He set the kettle down to gather his son into his arms. His tad always smelled of coffee and pipe smoke—the one he hid in the barn, thinking no one knew about it. "Christmas without you showed us a vision of life if we'd never had a son. I'd prefer to never experience it again."

"Stop *cwtching* in the kitchen and bring in the tea," his dad yelled out from the den. "C'mon, you two."

"Your dad."

Freddie grinned against the familiar flannel of his tad's shirt. "Your husband. Don't forget his biscuits."

"What have I said about mocking your father?"

"Only do it where he can hear?" Freddie's smile brightened further. He hoped he could take this for a sign his fathers would accept Taine in his life. "If you hold the door for me, I'll take the tray into the den."

His dads tried. They did. Freddie could almost see the effort they were going through to avoid having a repeat of Christmas.

The strained conversations eventually bled away into more genuinely cordial chatter. His dad's interest in rugby paved the way. He'd soon engaged Taine in a heated debate over the use of aggressively rolling mauls in a recent national team match.

"Turns out you only had to turn on the rugby to get them to ease up." His aunt sidled over to join him on the floor by the fire. She snatched a biscuit from his saucer. "Do I want to know what you two got up to in the shed that required a change of clothing?"

"No."

"You sure?"

"*No.*" Freddie glared at his aunt, who smiled in return. "Quit it."

"Anna, don't harass Freddie." His dad came to the rescue. "I haven't seen him blush so badly since we found naughty stories on his computer."

"Oh. My. God." Freddie shot to his feet, barely avoiding upending his tea. "Taine? Want to see the cows? We should go see them, right now. This very second. Let's go."

"Cows?" Taine chuckled the entire way out of the house into the brisk air and lightly falling snow. "Not interested in mooning animals, but I do want to hear more about these 'naughty stories' of yours. Did you write them?"

"*No,*" Freddie snapped at him. He could feel the blush spreading up his neck to his face and ears. "I'm going to kill them and feed them to the cows."

"Think it might affect the taste of the milk?"

"*Twmffat.*" He shoved Taine—or attempted to do so. The brick wall of a man didn't budge an inch. "I can't believe my dad brought it up. He went from hating you to embarrassing me rather quickly."

Taine grabbed him by the shoulders and massaged them firmly. "What sort of naughty stories were you reading?"

Freddie dropped his head forward with a groan. "*Doctor Who* fan fiction."

"Pardon?"

"You heard me." Freddie decided he'd rather crawl through the pasture full of cowpats than continue the conversation. "Stories written by fans of the *Doctor Who* show."

"Naughty ones?" Taine asked incredulously.

"Yes."

"And you're sure you didn't write any of them?" Taine shook him gently by the shoulders. "I think you did."

Freddie groaned as his answer. Taine turned him around to press him up against the wall of the barn. *Oh God, I can't sneak up to change my trousers again, they'll notice this time.* He didn't have a chance to voice his argument before the taller man's lips descended on his.

Taine licked a swath from Freddie's mouth up to his ear, teasing his earlobe with light nibbles. "Now, tell me all about the fantasies you used to write about. Maybe we can act out some of them."

"Why? Do you have a Tardis?" Freddie retorted sharply.

Silence.

"Well, not exactly, but I can promise it's bigger on the inside." Taine rested his head against Freddie's shoulder while they both broke into a fit of laughter. "Want to see my screwdriver?"

CHAPTER THIRTY-SIX

TAINE

Footsteps on the gravel outside the barn had Taine releasing Freddie. They stepped away from each other quietly, moving towards one of the nearby stalls. He watched while the younger man checked the feed for the cows.

"I hope you're both fully clothed." Adam Whittle entered the barn with one hand across his eyes. He peeked through his fingers with exaggerated caution. "Oh good, I won't have to bludgeon you to death with a shovel."

Taine stared the man down. He'd reached the conclusion that Freddie should be in his life no matter the age difference. Ridiculous comments weren't going to chase him away now. "I like my chances."

Adam smiled at him with less of an edge this time. "It's getting too cold to be out in this. Why don't you come in the house for some more tea?"

By the end of the day, Taine wanted nothing more than to return to the comforts of his own home. *With Freddie.* Cordial conversation grated on the nerves after a while. He didn't particularly want to relive his glory days either.

Sleeping in Freddie's childhood bed didn't sit well with him. *Well,* if Taine were completely honest with himself, the more perverse part of his personality did find it appealing. He doubted the younger man would've slept with anyone else there.

Gags might be required to silence both of us.

"I've no clue what idea has popped into your filthy mind, but whatever it is, the answer is no," Freddie whispered on his way to the kitchen from the dining table. They'd enjoyed leftovers from the Christmas roast. "Is your mind always in the gutter?"

"No. If it were, I'd be Scottie." Taine winked at Freddie, who rolled his eyes with exaggerated exasperation. "Need a hand with the clearing up?"

"Keep your hands to yourself in the mood you're in." Freddie gave what looked like a slightly worried glance towards his fathers, who appeared oblivious to the whispered conversation. "Can you behave yourself for one night?"

Taine couldn't help the wicked smirk on his face—he truly couldn't. "Can you? Wrapped up all warm next to me in bed?"

"*Taine.*" Freddie punched him on the shoulder before quickly disappearing into the kitchen, muttering under his breath in Welsh.

"Well, you've certainly discombobulated my nephew." Anna slid into the chair next to his. "I know the two of you have only known each other for a few months. We've done Freddie a disservice, I think, threatening you. He sees so much in his work. Maybe what he needs is someone strong enough to help him through the dark nights. He hides it, you see, from all of us."

"He does." Taine nodded respectfully and excused himself from the table.

Wandering down the hall, Taine paused at what clearly was the family gallery. Pictures lined both sides of the wall. He chuckled at the obligatory photo of Freddie in the bath— covered up to his chin in bubbles.

By midnight, it became painfully and hilariously obvious that Adam and Fred Whittle weren't comfortable at all with their adult son sharing a bed with someone under their roof. The evening dragged on and on while they created one excuse after the other. Taine wondered if he'd be trekking out to the inn for the night.

"Enough." Freddie called a halt to everything at half past. He rubbed his fingers vigorously through his hair, fighting a yawn. "We don't want to play charades. We don't want to watch anything on the telly. I certainly can't listen to another story about the old days. I'm going to bed. Taine's sleeping in it with me, which should prove interesting given the size of the mattress."

"That's us told." Adam lifted his eyebrows and exchanged a glance with his husband. "Well, good night. Please, for the sake of my heart, no odd noises."

"Odd noises?" Freddie stood slowly and kissed his fathers. "Night."

The confidence in Freddie's posture evaporated once they entered his room. He closed and locked his door before sinking on the bed. Taine leaned against the desk across from the mattress to watch while the younger man fought with the laces of his shoes.

Taine crouched down and caught the flailing fingers. "Why are you all wound up?"

"You know why." Freddie collapsed on his back to stare up at the ceiling. He didn't so much as twitch when Taine began to loosen the knotted laces. "If my fathers—"

"I'll keep you quiet." He pulled off the trainers and socks, tossing them to the side. His fingers gripped Freddie by the thighs to shift him closer to the edge of the bed. "Unless you'd rather wake the house with your shouts?"

"Don't be an arse." Freddie almost perfectly mimicked his slight Scottish lilt. He made a feeble attempt at dissuading Taine's fingers from unbuckling his belt. "We could always stay at the inn."

Taine dragged his thumb across the row of buttons covering Freddie's growing problem. "I do believe your body is speaking volumes to me."

The stream of Welsh that poured from Freddie's mouth had a decidedly blue streak to it. Taine smirked at him, pressing his thumb down enough to elicit a groan. He squeezed a few times and leaned up on his knees.

"What—"

Taine took a spare set of boxers that he'd grabbed from his bag earlier. He balled them up and shoved them in Freddie's mouth when he started to speak. "If you need to say yellow or red, spit the boxers out, all right?"

Freddie nodded.

Making quick work of stripping Freddie out of his clothes, Taine lifted him further up on the mattress. He glanced around the room and found several neckties hanging from a hook on the wall. *Perfect.* They'd work perfectly to restrain the nurse.

With his younger lover trussed up like the most sumptuous holiday meal, Taine stood at the foot of the bed to enjoy the visual. A plan of attack would definitely be required. He didn't want a quick bite of toast—this should be a buffet of sexually decadent indulgence.

Taine trailed his fingers along the sole of Freddie's foot absently while considering the options. He chuckled darkly when the restrained man wiggled in response immediately. "Are you ticklish, Frederick?"

Taine teased him for several seconds, eventually stopping, not wanting to turn it from fun into torture. A little could go a long way where sex was concerned. He had the man tied up on his hands and knees. *Why waste my time tickling him?*

Despite his earlier comments, it wouldn't be wise to draw the attention of everyone else in the house. Spanking and anything likely to make excessive noise would have to wait until they'd reached the privacy of his home. *Oh, oh the things I'll do to Freddie when I have all my toys.* He settled now for the thrill of having the younger man at his mercy.

And, I don't have condoms anyway.

Bollocks.

A glance around the childhood room of Freddie's told him the odds of finding a condom within it were slim to none. *Or lube.* Creativity would clearly be the name of the game. Taine took a closer look at the objects in the room and finally spotted the perfect one.

"Don't go anywhere." Taine grabbed a handful of permanent markers. He darted into the en suite to thoroughly wash them with warm water and soap. A tub of coconut oil caught his attention from where it rested on the counter. "*Brilliant.*"

From previous experience, he knew rubbing the coconut oil in his hand would give him a safe lube-like substance to use. It would work perfectly for his plans. He returned to the room with markers and the tub in his hand.

With his head down towards the bed, Freddie wouldn't be able to see much of anything. Taine grabbed a third necktie to use as a makeshift blindfold. He loved the way removing a sense intensified the others.

With Freddie unable to see, Taine began his work. He stretched out on his side on the mattress, sliding so his head slipped underneath the younger man's chest. Those pink nipples required careful attention.

Allowing his hot breath to waft across one then the other, Taine waited for the nubs to harden. It didn't take long. He latched on to a nipple with his teeth—tongue flicking against it.

The response came almost immediately. Freddie arched against Taine. He continued worrying his nipples.

Soft. Hard. Softer. Harder.

The varied licks and bites drew different levels of reaction from the younger man. Taine wondered idly if Freddie might enjoy clamps. He had some in his arsenal at home; he'd have to remember to try them.

Taine reached underneath Freddie with one hand to firmly grip his cock. He stroked hard. Once. Twice. He used his free fingers to pinch the hard, pink nub on his chest.

He held on tightly while Freddie bucked against him, causing himself additional pain from yanking on his nipple. "Am I not tweaking you hard enough, Frederick?"

Between working his nipples and his shaft, Taine drew out Freddie's climax easily enough. He stroked his thighs and sides gently. His own arousal was ignored for the moment while the younger man struggled for air.

Taine waited until he finally caught his breath. "Don't worry, Freddie. I'm not even close to being done with you yet."

CHAPTER THIRTY-SEVEN

FREDDIE

By the time the sun came up the next morning, Freddie discovered how many markers could be used to drive him to the brink of insanity. The offending items lay innocently on the floor by the bed when he slid out from under Taine's arm to get up. He tiptoed from the room to grab an early bath.

His ability to make it through breakfast depended on being clean and clothed. *Fully. Clothed.* He took comfort in knowing they wouldn't be spending another night under his parents' roof. Awkward didn't even begin to cover how he felt.

It also didn't explain why the thought of last night was enough to liven up his thirsty ferret.

"Behave yourself." Freddie frowned down at himself. "Oh, oh. This is great. I'm talking to myself."

A quick hot shower did him a world of good. He dressed quickly, trying not to wake the sleeping giant in his bed. His intention to get to the kitchen before anyone else failed miserably when he found his aunt by the hob.

"Morning." She drew the word out while pouring a mug of coffee for him. "You were rather silent last night. Did we behave ourselves?"

"Always." Freddie grabbed the mug and disappeared out of the kitchen.

"That's not a yes, Freddie."

He ignored his aunt shouting after him. Her laughter followed him through the house. He holed up by the fireplace— the only truly warm spot in the old place.

Dear coffee, I adore you. Not as much as cheese, but it's close. Please save me from my idiotic family who are going to want to embarrass me. Love, Freddie.

With his mental letter penned, Freddie sipped the slightly bitter liquid. He cupped the mug with both hands and brought it up to allow the steam to waft across his face. *I shagged in my childhood bed last night.*

He giggled.

"What are you cackling about in here?" His dad stumbled into the room in his pyjamas. "You're too happy this early in the morning."

Freddie grinned when he continued on his way, likely to the kitchen for coffee. After breakfast, he intended to make his excuses to start for Cardiff. He definitely wouldn't be staying another night under the same roof as his parents with Taine in bed with him.

His heart couldn't take the stress even if other parts of his anatomy found it thrilling. It could be excited in Cardiff as well as Cornwall. He didn't have a humiliation fetish.

I don't.

At all.

The morning went quickly. Before Freddie knew it, he stood outside in the sleet by his Mini. Taine had already swanned off to the inn, leaving him to deal with his fathers on his own.

He made it away from the farm without tears, lectures, or being smothered to death by *cwtch*. A win. The incredibly enormous crate of cheese, beer, and leftovers sitting in the back had been forced on him on the way out. His fathers apparently believed their son never bought groceries—or ate without being prompted.

Freddie made one stop on the way home to Cardiff to check on Genevieve. She happily accepted half of the treats from his dads by way of thanks for taking care of his cat. They exchanged presents, gossip, and drinks long into the evening.

The doctor's giggles over his being stuck at his family farm with Taine had Freddie calling it a night. Genevieve made him promise to bring coffee in the morning for both of them on their early shift. He left quickly before she could ask him anything else about the holidays.

She didn't need to know everything.

Collapsing on his couch, Freddie balled up a piece of paper to toss to Bitsy, who immediately pounced on it. He couldn't dredge up the energy to fix himself supper or do anything other than watch the muted telly. His flat had never seemed more cold and lonely.

The time had come to face facts. Taine had made a tangible and likely permanent impact on his world. Freddie wouldn't be brushing it off as a casual connection.

Taine had arrived in his life at the perfect moment. Stress from working with terminally ill patients had weighed heavily on his spirit. Freddie hadn't realised quite how much it impacted him until being around the Scottish Maori god forced him to relax.

All of it had blinded him to the truth that was slowly creeping up on his heart. He wanted Taine, more than simply lusting after the man's wicked body. They could have something special and long-lasting.

"Will Taine want me for more than a few sweaty, exhausting nights?" Freddie bent forward to ask Bitsy, who batted the paper at him. He decided to take the meow as a positive response to his question. "Yes, yes, I'll throw your new toy for you."

CHAPTER THIRTY-EIGHT

TAINE

"Are you still thinking about fucking the nurse?" Scottie dodged the fist Taine launched in his direction. "Oi! Arsehole. I was only asking. You're moping around like some—"

"Why don't you sod off before his fist connects with your jaw and breaks it?" Caddock grabbed Scottie by the back of the shirt and slung him around towards the hallway. "Go sit outside and think about what you've done."

"Yes, mum," Scottie grumbled.

"Why's he our mate?" BC joined them in the library, pouring glasses of whisky for all of them. "You can laugh, but I'm serious. Why do we put up with him?"

"We put up with you, don't we?" Caddock easily avoided BC's kick. His gaze shifted over to Taine after a moment.

"You could make it to Cardiff by midnight."

"And? I've done one mad dash this holiday already." Taine attempted an indifferent shrug, but the dubious looks from his friends told him he'd failed. "It doesn't matter."

"Yeah, pull the other one." BC snatched the drink out of his hand before Taine could even get a first sip. "Have a coffee and a sandwich then get your arse on the road to see Freddie. We can all see you want to, Tens."

"If this past year taught me anything, it's that life is far too short to piss away a chance at something special." Graham snagged the spare tumbler of whisky. "Don't spit love in the eye before it's even truly begun."

"He read that on a fortune cookie in Shanghai," BC teased his boyfriend, who rolled his eyes in response. "If you don't go, I'll tell Mrs Morgan you volunteered to help her clean up after Scottie."

"Right." Taine decided not to test whether or not his friend was bluffing. He'd seen Scottie's hotel rooms in the past, and slob didn't even come close to describing the man. "You're all knobheads, and I hate you."

Three coffees, two sandwiches, and one drive to Cardiff later, Taine began to question his own sanity. He'd decided about halfway through the journey that Freddie would be coming home with him. It was time to play out some of his more lurid fantasies.

Taine knocked on the door, trying to walk the line between waking Freddie and not annoying his neighbours. He couldn't help smiling at the tousled hair and sleepy eyes on the pyjama-clad nurse. "Is your pussycat good to spend a night alone?"

Freddie scratched his side absently while rubbing his eyes with his other hand. He blinked groggily up at Taine. "Is this a kidnapping?"

"Only for a night," Taine promised.

"You drove all the way from Cornwall in the middle of the night to ask me to sleep at your house? What's with you and the odd driving times? It couldn't have waited until a normal hour?" Freddie rested his head against the door and yawned widely. "Why?"

"Just pack a bag, Frederick." Taine wondered if it would actually require kidnapping to move things along more quickly. "I'll get you the good coffee for breakfast."

"Promise?"

With much grumbling and shuffling of feet, the normally cheerful Freddie stumbled along beside Taine all the way to his vehicle. The drive to his place went quietly and quickly. His passenger snored through most of it.

His plans would clearly have to wait for morning. Taine led the drowsy Freddie into his bedroom, stripped him down to his pants, and tucked him under the covers. After checking on Speedy, he quickly unpacked and showered before sliding into bed behind his younger lover.

Sleeping with a hard cock and vivid, active imagination was nigh impossible. Taine barely managed to doze. His waking moments, however, provided ample time to plot out all sorts of debauchery before breakfast.

"Wide awake, I see." Freddie's voice was filled with humour. He shifted slightly, rubbing himself against Taine's arousal. "Been up long?"

"All sodding night." Taine bent his head to catch Freddie's neck with his teeth, biting and sucking hard enough to leave a mark. He teased the now tender skin, which caused Freddie to hiss at him. "Let's get you in the shower."

"I don't smell," Freddie muttered suspiciously. "Why are we taking a shower?"

"No, you don't, but I plan on taking you against the tile wall before I spank your arse until you're overheating and begging for more." Taine slid a hand roughly into the top of Freddie's boxers to grab a hold of his semihard shaft. "Have I got your attention, Frederick? Fuck yourself into my hand. Show me how much you want me."

"*Twmffat.*"

Taine waited until he felt a change in Freddie's pace. He stretched a hand out to grab a cock ring from the nightstand and clapped it around his lover's heavy arousal. "Let's get washed up."

Ignoring Freddie's questions about the toy now restricting him, Taine dragged him into the shower. Thirty minutes in the shower were enough to teach his lover the exquisite pain of being unable to reach the pinnacle of release. He heaped injury to insult by stroking himself to completion across Freddie's chest while he knelt on the tile floor.

A brilliant start to the day.

Now I get to redden his arse all I want.

The rest had to be set up perfectly. Taine didn't necessarily live the bondage lifestyle—he dabbled. All of his toys and equipment could be used in and out of a scene for that reason.

Of everything in the world of BDSM, Taine's true fetish

lay in erotic spanking. Several years ago, he'd invested in a vintage wooden sawhorse. It had been fitted with padded leather cushions and rings along the struts.

Most of the time the sawhorse acted as a place to toss his clothing at night. Taine cleared it off and easily dragged it into the centre of the bedroom. Freddie watched him with a mixture of curiosity and lust evident in his eyes.

"Red, yellow, or green?" Taine held a gag in one hand and a set of leather restraints in the other. "Can I show you the level of my debauchery?"

Freddie grinned at him before staring pointedly at the restraints. "You're asking me?"

"I might hold the ropes, but all the power rests in your consent." Taine dragged the tip of the silicone penis-shaped gag against the tip of Freddie's shaft. "Pick a colour, Frederick."

"Green." Freddie moaned out the word. "Were you a sodding medieval torturer in a past life?"

"The torture hasn't even begun." Taine smiled wickedly at him. He smeared the small gag across the moisture leaking from Freddie's arousal and then pressed it into his lover's mouth. The straps easily went around his head where Taine carefully secured it. "I'll put a cloth in your hand. Drop it if you switch to yellow or red."

Freddie nodded his understanding, lips shifting around the silicone. Life generally went by in a rush, so Taine enjoyed the methodical pleasure of restraining someone across his custom-made bench. It didn't take long to have him comfortably secured.

Taine ran his fingers along the crease of Freddie's arse.

"I've dreamt of having you here—all tied up and at my mercy. And oh, Frederick, the mercy I'm going to show you."

While his fingers gently explored the creamy flesh, Taine's eyes strayed to the few spanking accoutrements laid out on the nearby dresser. Where should he start? He wanted to ensure Freddie enjoyed every moment.

"I'm starting you off with my favourite." Taine skated the tip of the leather crop across Freddie's back. "Maybe we'll add a clamp or a plug next time—I've so much to show you."

Beginning with a light massage to warm the skin up, Taine lulled Freddie into relaxing against the leather padding. The first swat was light and caught the lower part of his arse. His lover moaned around the gag when his body jerked against his binding.

Any movement from Freddie would grind his arousal against the bench. Taine had made sure of it. As the force of the swats increased, his lover would wind up practically humping the leather.

Soft.

Hard.

Soft.

Hard.

Taine could feel the heat on Freddie's arse, and eventually, he set the crop aside. He snagged an ice cube from the nearby cup of water. The shock of the cold on his skin set his sexual captive writhing madly.

Minutes ticked by. Icy drops dripped along sensitive skin. Taine revelled in the joy of indulging himself with a man he felt such a connection with.

All the playing throughout the early morning hours had pushed both of them as close to the brink as one could go without exploding. Taine snagged a condom and lube from a nearby drawer. He teased Freddie open with his fingers while dragging his long length across his lover's arse.

With no worries about being heard, Taine thrust his condom-covered shaft into the lubricated tightness of his lover. He waited until his climax was close before reaching underneath to release Freddie from the cock ring. They cried out together not long after.

Taine made sure not to crush Freddie against the bench while catching his breath. "God, you're brilliant."

If one could make a moan sound snarky, Freddie managed it around the gag. Taine laughed. He had to before carefully easing himself out and tossing the used condom to the side.

With gentle hands, Taine released Freddie and carried him over to the bed. He used a warm flannel to clean both of them up. With that handled, he grabbed a bottle of lotion to apply some to those spanked cheeks.

"Aftercare is important. Up you get." Taine eased Freddie up and handed him a cup of water. "Drink. You need it."

Freddie collapsed on the bed after his drink. "I shouldn't be so tired after sleeping."

"I'm just that good." Taine sank down on the mattress beside him and smiled when Freddie rolled over to rest his head on his chest. "Have any plans for New Year's Eve? Or Easter? How about St Valentine's Day? Next Christmas?"

Freddie tilted his head until their eyes met. "Bit early to worry about next Christmas, isn't it? No plans so far. Why?"

"I've decided to block out all the important dates on your calendar." Taine spoke more firmly than he felt inside. He didn't want to allow anyone else to have the chance to come between them. "One more important question. How does your cat feel about hamsters?"

"Good with brown sauce."

Taine stared down at the brown-haired nurse before bursting into laughter. "Knobhead."

Perfection, Taine decided, was Freddie beside him. If every morning and evening ended this way, he could die a happy, satisfied man. Now, he only had to work hard to ensure it never changed.

How hard can it be?

EPILOGUE

Winter and spring had flown by for Freddie. Life had been altered dramatically for him on so many levels—good, brilliant, and not-so-great changes. Taine had been at his side through all of it.

Cuts across the NHS had affected the hospitals in Cardiff as well. Freddie lost his beloved job in late February. He moped for a week until Taine gave him a brilliant idea—offer his skills to one of the many cancer charities.

A month of research and interviews followed until finally, Freddie started working with Tenovus Cancer Care as a nurse advisor in their chemo callback service. He found himself enjoying the work greatly. The only thing he missed about the hospital was Genevieve, and he saw her at least once a week for coffee.

As for Taine, they saw each other at least four nights out of the week—one of the benefits of having a more stable job that didn't require his travelling all over the country. Their friends expected them to move in together. Freddie didn't think they would for at least another year; they both appreciated having the option of space, even if they usually ended up sleeping together more often than not.

At the beginning of the year, Taine had started assisting with the training for one of the Cardiff rugby teams. He'd also spent a lot of time keeping Scottie from losing his mind with renovating the nightclub. The Sin Bin would have its soft opening for friends and family next week, so today they'd be walking through it with Francis, who had handled the design.

Taine, Scottie, Caddock, BC, and Remi had been the main investors of the club, along with a few of their other former teammates. As only two of them lived in Cardiff, the others had relied on Taine and Scottie to handle any issues with renovating the property they'd purchased. It had made for an exhausting six months.

"Ready?"

Freddie glanced over at Taine, who was driving them over to the club. "No."

"Scottie promised to be nice. Caddock had words with him when he got in Francis's face." Taine dropped a hand on his knee to squeeze. "I know he's an arsehole."

"I imagine Francis had words with him, as well." He grinned at Taine. For being a bit mild-mannered, they'd learned never to underestimate the interior designer. "Not much else to say, is there?"

They pulled up outside the Sin Bin. It appeared to be nothing more than an old building that had once been part of a wharf. They'd kept the exterior almost completely intact. Only those in the know would be showing up at the club.

A secret den of iniquity.

Scottie hadn't liked Francis's description. Everyone else had loved the concept. Old wharf on the outside, lush leather and smoky colours on the inside of the nightclub. The three-storey building offered a bar on one level, a dance floor on another, and space for live music.

"What crawled up Scottie's arse?" Freddie glanced around at the dark blue walls, leather chairs, old carpets, and artwork on the walls that looked like they'd fit into a prohibition bar. "It's brilliant."

"It's too *gay.*" Taine mimicked Scottie's gravelly and coarse voice perfectly.

Freddie paused in his inspection of a row of framed photos of former rugby players; much of the décor also had a sports vibe to it. "Scottie does realise that he's as bent as we are, right? He also realises most of the advertising has been touting this as a gay club—or at least gay friendly."

"He does."

Freddie shook his head in disbelief. "Unbelievable."

"Francis hasn't arrived yet." Taine glanced around the room. "Are we early?"

Heading out of the club, Freddie strolled across the road to stand by the railing looking across the water. The summer thus far had been mild. He hoped the evening of the opening would be the same.

Taine moved up behind him, wrapping his arms around Freddie and resting their heads together. "Are you happy?"

"I'm always happy." Freddie elbowed Taine in the side when his arms squeezed too tightly. "I'm still not moving in with you."

"I didn't ask." He rubbed his rough beard against Freddie's neck. "Don't be naughty, Frederick, I'll have to spank you."

"You'll do that anyway," Freddie retorted. He gripped the railing in front of him while his thoughts turned to something more serious. "Genevieve rang me yesterday. She's taking a sabbatical from the hospital to join a non-profit group of doctors. They're going to Yemen for a month starting in August."

"Thinking of going?" Taine's arms once again tightened around him.

"Remember Hamish?"

"The retired Royal Marine who works private security?" Taine asked after a prolonged silence. "Didn't he get into a fight with Scottie at the party the other night?"

"That's the one. Genevieve's mother hired him to travel with her, so we'll have extra security." Freddie hadn't talked to his dads or aunt about it yet. They wouldn't want him to go, but he could make a difference, even if it were only for a short time. His boss at the charity had already tentatively approved the time off; they'd be sending several nurses, actually. "It's a month."

"I'll worry." Taine twisted Freddie around in his arms, pressing him up against the railing. "You'll have to bring

Bitsy so I can keep an eye on her."

"You don't mind my going?"

Taine frowned at him. "Not my job to mind. I'm here to offer support and encouragement. That's what you do for someone you love."

"Love?" Freddie blinked up at him. He might've thought the word a few times, but he'd certainly never said it. "Did you—"

Taine cut him off with a hard kiss. "I love you."

Freddie ran his tongue across his swollen lips and tried to force his mind to function. "You aren't just saying this because you're afraid I might not come back from Yemen?"

"Don't be a knobhead, Frederick." Taine bit the tip of his nose.

He grinned up at the tall man looming over him. "I love you too."

"Good. *Brilliant.*" Taine's lips twisted into a blinding smile. "Let's invite this Hamish to the opening next week. I want to impress upon him the importance of you returning to me safely."

"And the fact that he's going to piss Scottie off?"

"Added bonus." Taine pressed up against Freddie. "I'll miss you, Frederick."

"For a month." Freddie didn't think it would be that much of a hardship. "Thirty days isn't anything to cry over."

Taine brought his hands up to cup Freddie's face. His thumb scratched at the short stubble on his face. "I *love* you, and I'll miss you."

"*Fi'n caru ti.*" Freddie tilted his head up for a soft kiss that seemed to go on forever. He repeated himself in English, so there was no mistake. "I love you."

THE END

WELSH TRANSLATIONS

Drewgi - skunk

Twmffats - idiots

Coc y gath - The Cat's Willy (Or - Bollocks)

Cachu hwch - Pig's Poo (It's all gone Wrong)

Dim gwerth rhech dafad - not worth a sheep's fart

 (completely useless)

Tad - Dad

S'mae - How are you?

Cwtch - cuddle

Cariad/Caru - sweetheart/love

Diawl bach - little devil

Bara Brith - a traditional Welsh fruit loaf.

Cach - shit

Fi'n caru ti - I love you

ACKNOWLEDGMENTS

A massive thank you to my betas, Becky, Olivia and all the brilliant people at Hot Tree, and my beloved hubby who didn't complain too much about my hunting for attractive men on Instagram for book inspiration.

Thanks to all of my readers, whether this is the first or fourth of my stories that you've read. Hope you enjoy Freddie & Tens adventure as much as I did.

ABOUT THE AUTHOR

Dahlia Donovan wrote her first romance series after a crazy dream about shifters and damsels in distress. She prefers irreverent humour and unconventional characters.

An autistic and occasional hermit, her life wouldn't be complete without her husband and her massive collection of books and video games.

Stay connected with Dahlia:

Facebook: www.facebook.com/dahliadonovan

Website: www.dahliadonovan.com

Twitter: www.twitter.com/DahliaDonovan

MORE FROM DAHLIA:

Gay Romance

After the Scrum

The Wanderer (The Sin Bin #1)

The Caretaker (The Sin Bin #2)

The Botanist (The Sin Bin #2.5)

Found You (Trade Me Novella)

Paranormal Romance

The Misguided Confession

ABOUT THE PUBLISHER

Hot Tree Publishing opened its doors in 2015 with an aspiration to bring quality fiction to the world of readers. With the initial focus on romance and a wide spread of romance sub-genres, they envision opening up to alternative genres in the near future.

Firmly seated in the industry as a leading editing provider to independent authors and small publishing houses, Hot Tree Publishing is the sister company to Hot Tree Editing, founded in 2012. Having established in-house editing and promotions, plus having a well-respected market presence, Hot Tree Publishing endeavours to be a leader in bringing quality stories to the world of readers.

Interested in discovering more amazing reads brought to you by Hot Tree Publishing or perhaps you're interested in submitting a manuscript and joining the HTPubs family? Either way, head over to the website for information:

WWW.HOTTREEPUBLISHING.COM